George Henry Miles

Loretto

Or, the choice

George Henry Miles

Loretto
Or, the choice

ISBN/EAN: 9783337422820

Printed in Europe, USA, Canada, Australia, Japan

Cover: Foto ©Andreas Hilbeck / pixelio.de

More available books at **www.hansebooks.com**

LORETTO; OR, THE CHOICE.

BY GEORGE H. MILES.

A New, Revised, and Enlarged Edition.

BOSTON:
THOMAS B. NOONAN & CO.
17, 19, AND 21 BOYLSTON STREET.
1883.

LORETTO;

OR, THE CHOICE.

CHAPTER I.

THERE once was — where many may still remember — a neat farmhouse, not large, but tastefully built, with dormer windows projecting from the high, sharp roof and a double portico running around it. It was a venerable house, rather emblematic of comfort than affluence, beautifully situated on the cleared slope of a well-wooded hill. In winter it was somewhat dreary to those who passed and knew not the fireside joys within; but in summer the birds and the flowers, the vines and honeysuckles, peopled with busy bees and festooning the porches, the rich herbage rolling over the fertile plain, until, changing color in the distance, it grew blue as the vault it seemed to kiss, the elms, the oaks, and the maples, all united to make *Loretto* — for so it was called — a little Eden.

A clear, quick trout-stream ran through the lawn to the north, giving that fine finish to the landscape which running water only can impart. In the misty spring mornings at break of day you could always see, looming through the fog along this stream, an elderly man, with a broad felt hat drawn over his cheeks to keep' off the flies, dressed in a close-bodied gray coat and breeches of permanent pepper and salt. He was tall and portly, and though not absolutely lame, there was a decided halt in his gait, injuring its grace, perhaps, but sparing its dignity. There he could always be found during the choicest hours of the legitimate season, with his rod fast in hand and all his tackle around him, fishing away with so much temper and so little skill that rare, indeed, was it when the proprietor of Loretto breakfasted on trout of his own catching.

But the Colonel never angled alone; in spite of old Isaac he was far too wise for that. A bright-faced mulatto boy named Charley was his inseparable companion in all these matinal excursions. From his own intuitive sagacity of internal organization, and from careful study of his master's mistakes, Charley had become an expert in the art in which his preceptor remained a bungler. Whilst the Colonel bustled about to the mortal terror of every fish within twenty yards of his fly, Charley, breathless in the bushes, patiently cast his wriggling earthworm and drew out with a quiet smile the unsuspecting victims that dreaded the more tempting bait.

The Colonel was never jealous. So completely had he merged Charley's individuality in his own, that the idea of Charley's having caught a fish never entered into his speculations — it was perfectly ridiculous. Why, Charley belonged to him quite as much as his own hair line — and what mattered it whether he used his tapering English tube, or his less elastic black boy as a rod — for Charley was but a rod in the case — all the difference being that one was of foreign, the other of native origin. Over and over again, when not a trout had twirled his reel, and when a dozen noble prisoners floundered in the tin-pan at the little fellow's heels, would the Colonel, eyeing the speckled beauties as their clear scales glittered in the sun, exclaim, " Ah, you little rogues, you could not escape me ! " And so firmly was the Colonel persuaded of this that to all the juries in the county he would have sworn that *he* had caught those fish. This was one of the Colonel's eccentricities — failing would be too hard a name for his innocent and confirmed delusion; and so fervently did he believe it that

Charley himself was to the full as certain of the proposition as his master, and would have resented any insinuation of the truth as a most unfounded calumny.

Through all the country round the proprietor of Loretto was a favorite; men, women, and children celebrated the purity and benevolence of his character, and, as is frequently done, magnified even his peculiarities into virtues. At wedding, christening, and wake he was the principal man in all the neighborhood; in all matters of etiquette an oracle. If any doubtful point of precedence occurred, if any knotty question of honor arose, if any nice shade of interest was to be decided, on which the doubtful light of the law was unsolicited, — the Colonel was sure to be invoked; and he gave his responses forth with so much sagacity, sincerity, and pointed brevity, that his reputation rose with every decision, and he stood arbitrator *par excellence* for the country. Even his title, the Colonel, was a mark rather of love and honor than of any military service, past or present. True it was that in the late war he had been captain of a company, and that his knee had been stiffened by an enemy's ball, — but this had happened long ago, and his gallantry, though noticed in the prints of the day, was all unchronicled in history.

The Colonel was a bachelor — but he did not live alone; his sister Mary divided with him the empire of Loretto. Mrs. Cleveland was under fifty — some ten years younger than her brother. She was a shade over the medium size of woman — rather slightly made, and her shoulders curved a little forward by weakness or care. Her hair, which she wore drawn straight from her forehead behind her ear, was in blended lines of black and white; her eye was large, calm, and clear, — the expression of her face habitually sad and reserved. There were lines of thought and determination about her mouth, but smoothed and softened as if the hand of resignation had touched them. She had the true mother-look in which infant innocence first reposes, and which manly virtue most reveres. Her brother loved her more than his life, and well was his love returned. She knew how to ward off his occasional fits of petulance, and how to meet them, when, in spite of her, they came in momentary gustiness. Loretto was a happy house, and especially happy when the third and last of the family left the convent school, whose small spire just rose above the neighboring woods, — when she left the good sisters and young friends with whom her youth had gone by like a sweet, sweet dream, to join her own family circle and spend the year — the whole year — winter and summer, ay, life itself, so it seemed, at Loretto.

Agnes Cleveland had just completed her studies at the convent, — she had gone through the prescribed course brilliantly and well, — she had stayed even a year beyond the required time — and now there was nothing more to be learned, nothing more to be gained by remaining. At least, so thought the world and the Colonel.

She left school in the bright month of July, with the blessing of all who knew her, with her tears falling fast on the load of honors she held with difficulty in both arms. She had always left before at the same season to spend the summer at home: but then it was different, — *then* it was only for a short vacation — then the future was to be but a repetition of the past, filled with the same well-known faces, endeared by the same innocent pastimes, hallowed by the same tranquil pursuits, and sanctified by the same long sweet prayers — by Mass in the morning, by Angelus at noon, by Litany at night. At first she did not feel the change so keenly. It was impossible to realize that there was no return to the convent — that her desk was to have another occupant, her flower-bed another mistress; but when the summer melted into gorgeous autumn, and she still remained at

Loretto, when she felt that her *heart* was to be changed before she could forget the girl and become a woman, her tears were less frequent, indeed, but far more painful.

She endeavored to conceal her sadness from her mother and uncle, but it was too plain. It puzzled and annoyed the Colonel — she had always been so cheerful, so free from all the melancholy of thought, though thoughtful too. He never inquired the cause, but his conjectures were multitudinous and incessant.

It was a bright winter afternoon — the snow was lying deep and well-beaten over the road, just hardening after the midday thaw, as the sun went down without a cloud about him. Agnes had returned with her mother from vespers at the convent chapel. They were sitting silently in the twilight before the generous wood-fire that kept the parlor bright and warm. The Colonel had gone to take an airing on horseback, as he phrased it, which, in other words, was a visit of benediction to the poor.

For many minutes they sat, each steadily gazing into the fire, which sparkled and crackled as though it loved and welcomed them.

"Agnes," said Mrs. Cleveland at last, without raising her eyes, "you must be unhappy."

There was a long pause, and the fire burned

loudly, and the sigh of the wind was plainly heard from without.

"Are you not?" asked the mother, for the first time hazarding a look at her daughter.

Agnes was leaning back in her chair; her head thrown forward almost on her breast; her hands clasped and resting between her knees, her tears glancing down her cheeks.

"Are you not?" repeated Mrs. Cleveland, touching her straightened arms.

The touch was electric. Without a word, the young girl rose and cast herself on her mother's bosom.

"I am! I am!" she sobbed again and again. "Oh, mother!" she said, "I love you, and yet I wish to leave you — I must leave you!" she added with more energy, kissing her parent's pale forehead as she spoke.

"Leave me for what, Agnes?" said Mrs. Cleveland, smoothing her daughter's hair, which had fallen loose in her agitation.

"For the convent!"

Louder and louder burned the fire, and louder was the sigh of the wind without.

Mrs. Cleveland was not unprepared for this; she had long since read her daughter's heart. The habitual half-smile of quiet resignation played around her lips. Agnes was surprised at her calmness.

"And you would really leave me then, my child?" resumed the mother, tenderly pressing the small hand she had taken in hers.

"Leave you for God alone!" said Agnes, "for God alone, mother. Do not think me insensible to all your goodness; do not doubt my love — you cannot, you do not doubt it! I have been unhappy because I dreaded your opposition, and knew the trial I was preparing for you; unhappy, because I was resisting an impulse which I recognized as from Heaven, and which, in spite of every human obstacle, I must obey!"

Mrs. Cleveland was still unmoved, or if there was any change it was only in her clear eye, in which the unshed tear hung and trembled; only in the slight movement of her lips, playing with a happier smile. "Have you spoken to your confessor?" she asked.

"I have."

"And"—

"He cautioned me against obeying an impulse which might only be transient; advising me to consider it more maturely."

"And I, my daughter, repeat his advice. Think not of me in your decision, but of your own immortal soul, of Him who will one day judge it, and of your spotless Mother, who sits in heaven exalted above the angels. Please her, and you will not fail to please me. You are young, and a few months in society may undermine your purpose. But, my own Agnes, you must be happy now — you have not pained me, nor can you ever pain me, my child, so long as you hold the call of God your first duty."

"Yes mother, I will be happy now; it will not cost an effort."

"God bless you!" Mrs. Cleveland held her daughter closer to her heart, and Colonel Cleverton entered the room.

"A quarrel and a reconciliation, I take it, ladies," he said, as he threw an enormous overcoat into a corner and took off his spurs. "Whew! this hill's as cold as an iceberg, and would freeze a polar bear, but for a friend like this," and he thrust both hands into the cheerful blaze that rose joyously to hail his coming. But though apparently unobservant, the Colonel had his eyes about him, and saw that he was just in at the close of a scene.

At tea he was struck with the altered manner of his niece. Her eyes would swim at times, but there was a world of joy in her face — of calm, deep, holy joy, joy that made him wonder.

After the cloth was removed, she lit his cigar with a smile such as he had not seen for many a day. She played backgammon with him until after nine, and, in the excitement of the game, her eyes glittered, her laugh rang, and she shook her hair from her temples as joyously as when he held her on his knee and gave her sweet things to win her love. And when the old mahogany clock struck ten, and she presented on one knee a brimming mug of brown October, —

"Agnes," said he, as the creaming ale touched his mouth, "thank God! you are yourself again."

Before the tankard descended, Agnes had left the room.

"Mary," began the old man, looking steadfastly at his sister, "is that young girl in love with any one but me?"

"Not that I am aware of."

"You have had a conversation with her," he continued, with the air of one who defies contradiction.

"I have."

"And you discovered the secret of her unhappiness?"

"Yes!"

"May I know it?"—this almost amounted to a challenge.

"Yes, brother, you had better know it at once. Agnes wishes to return to the convent."

The Colonel shuddered.

"To spend another year there?"

"To spend her life there!"

"As a nun?"

"Yes!"

"Good God!" thundered the Colonel, bounding from his chair and knocking his stick with terrible emphasis against the floor. "Agnes a nun! And you permit it, sister!" The old man paced rapidly up and down the room, whilst the perspiration gathered in large drops on his forehead. "You permit it! and sit there as contentedly as if she were going to a ball — and speak of it calmly — speak of it to *me* calmly — as if *I* had no heart — as if *I* could see the immolation of one of God's fairest creatures without a tear. Why, it would make me weep to chain up one of my hounds for life — but this young flower, this Agnes — madam, you are a stone!"

Mrs. Cleveland was silent.

"Oh, I did not think it of her!" muttered the Colonel, in vain attempting to arrest his tears, "I did not think it of her. To leave her old uncle — I who have loved her — loved her as age alone can love youth — I who have made myself a boy for her these fifteen years — to leave her old uncle — oh, this is bad enough! But to leave her mother" —

He stopped short and turned upon his sister with flashing eye and heaving breast : —

"Mary; is she not your child; your own, your only child, bone of your bone, flesh of your flesh; has she not your own image stamped upon her face; are you *not a mother*, and can you calmly see her cut down in her youth, her hopes and beauty blasted; can you calmly see her walking, a willing fanatic, into a dreary, lonely dungeon? Tell me, sister, can you see the axe descending on her neck, and smile like an Indian executioner? Tell me! — there is the same blood in our veins!" —

"But not the same faith in our hearts."

"And you consent, then?" stammered the Colonel, pale with passion.

"I do, brother, and hear me. There's nothing under Heaven so dear to me as Agnes. I lived for her when I would have died without her. I have nothing else on earth to love, save *you*, brother, save *you*, my best and first friend! But, if I find that I have nursed her for God and not for man, for the cloister and not for the cold, indecent, hollow-hearted ball-room, I tell you, brother, there's not a mother living, be she slave or be she queen, who will be as proud, as happy, as thankful as I."

"Ah! you are leagued to kill me. Strike. I

can bear no more!" He sank back in his chair.

"Did woman ever marry with a fairer chance of happiness than I? exclaimed Mrs. Cleveland, rising to her full height, whilst her face glowed. "Oh, I looked forward to a future such as few can fancy; and when I thought it in my reach, it turned to burning sand."

"There are few such villains as "—

"Hush! Man is too corrupt to be judged by his fellows. We need a more merciful tribunal," and she pointed above.

The Colonel paused a moment, then changed his tactics. "But this young creature, scarcely twenty, knows not her own mind; and I know of nothing more dangerous, more treacherous, more outrageously abominable, than to wrest this momentary inclination to her own destruction before she has time "—

"She shall have time!"

"How long?"

"One year."

CHAPTER II.

NE year!" muttered the Colonel to him-self, after Mrs. Cleveland had retired, drawing his capacious arm-chair closer to the fire as he spoke. His tears had dried, his face had cleared up, and presently his eye began to twinkle with a sly expression, as if some bright idea had suddenly crossed his mind.

"One year, eh?" he repeated audibly, smooth-ing his thin white hair; then, emptying the mug of ale mechanically, he threw his feet heavily upon the fender, rubbed his hands until they tingled, and chuckled, "I have it! I have it!"

The Colonel rose with that confident slowness with which a gentleman of the old school leaves the table, in the inspiration of the moment, to bring forth with his own hand his best bottle for his best friend. He opened the front door cautiously and stepped tiptoe on the portico. He paused a moment; it was a clear winter night, the frost had polished the stars, and their rays surrounded them like long eyelashes of gold. The cold wind refreshed him, and he drank it in like water.

"Oh, my dear little pet," he thought, "they shall never coop you up here from the sight of those blessed fields, among which you will ramble hereafter ! "

Then for the first time feeling that it was freezing hard, he crept on tiptoe to the door of a small room opening on the porch.

" Charley ! " he whispered shrilly through the keyhole.   In an instant came the answer, " Sir ! " A turn, a sigh, a shake ; the door was unbolted, and the little fellow's curly head appeared.

" Charley ! dress warm, saddle Fleetly for yourself, and come into the parlor.   Do it quietly."

The sagacious boy nodded, and the Colonel hobbled back.   He took his immense writing-desk from its time-honored green bag, unlocked it carefully, and selecting a quill, mended a pen with infinite pains.

Charley reappeared before the old gentleman had finished writing, and without saying a word, stood by the door.

" Get closer to the fire, my boy, closer ; warm up well," ejaculated the Colonel, looking to see that his commands were obeyed.

"There ! " he continued, describing a flourish after his name, folded the letter and sealed it.

" Are you warm, Charley ? "

" Yes, sir."

" Where's your great-coat, eh ? and comfort, eh ? Get them, you inconsiderate rascal ! Do you think I want to freeze you on Fleetly's back, to be a Christmas snow-man for the children of the neighborhood ? "

Charley retired, and the Colonel directed the letter. "Now you're all right — no, stop! your ear's out," and he fixed the comfort carefully, even tenderly, around the boy's neck and head. " Take this letter to the post-office; it must go at five by the morning mail. Be sure you drop it into the box and not the gutter, and mind you, Charley, not a word ! "

With a bow and a smile, the trusty messenger departed. When he had gone the Colonel again ensconced himself in his chair, and, contrary to custom, lit another cigar and replenished his mug. But he only drank half. He sat there until Charley returned, after performing his task in half an hour.

" Well-timed, my boy !   Is the letter in ? "

A nod.

" The horse attended to ? "

Another nod.

" Keep close to the fire then, and drink this: drink, I say ! it won't hurt you," said the Colonel, slapping him on the back.

In a few minutes more they were both abed; but long after Charley was snoring the Colonel kept tossing on his pillow, repeating —

"My sister, we are playing a long game of chess, and I have just made the first move!"

What the move was will soon appear.

If any are interested in the game let them follow; if placing the pieces has not been tedious, the moves, perchance, may please, or what is more, instruct.

It may be supposed that the Colonel was a Protestant; he was not, however. He was a Catholic, at least he had been a Catholic; but that was long ago, when his mother lived. By neglecting his religious duties for forty years he had imbibed all the prejudices of society, all the errors of humanitarianism, all the suggestions of indifferentism; in short, he was utterly decatholicized, and nothing more nor less than a thoroughbred man of the world, living for time and not for eternity, loving his neighbor as the world understands it, but neglecting his God.

Agnes was up with the sun and at mass. Her heart bounded gladly and fervently as she walked home with the bloom of health, youth, and piety on her cheeks. Summer never seemed fairer than that winter morning, and the sun on the snow-clad hill-tops told of brightness beyond its own, brightness beyond the grave. No birds were singing, but melody was all around her;

no flowers were blooming, but the air was fra-
grance, for her God was in her bosom, and her
mother leaned on her arm.

Breakfast and the Colonel were waiting for
them at Loretto. The Colonel was a scrupulous
observer of all the habits which bachelorship
invents and cherishes. One of these was to kiss
his niece before coffee every morning, when he
had the chance. But this time his embrace was
more affectionate than it had ever been, and
Agnes observed it.

Christmas was drawing near. Confectioners'
windows in the village were already bespangled
with visions that riveted the eyes and moistened
the mouths of troops of eager boys, who knew
that the second harvest of the year, the annual
feast, was coming. Agnes too looked forward to
it as a season of joy unbounded ; for her gift was
to be the divine child himself, who sanctified the
day.

Three days after the Colonel had written, an
answer came. It was brief and satisfactory:

"MY DEAR OLD UNCLE,
       "Expect this evening, yours,
                          "ELLEN ALMY."

"Bless her bright young soul!" exclaimed

the Colonel, pressing the paper to his heart. "Lel's the queen that will win this game!"

That day was the longest the Colonel had ever spent; it seemed to him as though evening would never come. He examined his tackle, his guns, his razors; he whistled, he sang, read, wrote, walked, rode; but do what he would, the hours were ages. By a strong effort, he managed to conceal his anxiety from his sister and niece; still they might have noticed that he started at the sound of every sleigh-bell, and that he took a particular pleasure in standing at the window. He was singularly musical, too, and there was scarce one ballad of the olden time from which the Colonel did not borrow a phrase in the course of the day.

Evening came at last, and with it Ellen Almy.

"Why, there's a sleigh at our gate," exclaimed Agnes, rising and going to the window.

"Who can it be?" said the Colonel, opening the door.

Agnes followed him out on the porch.

"Who are they, Aggie; your eyes are better than mine?"

"Strangers to me, a lady and gentleman."

Presently they heard a sweet, clear voice; "Yes, this is the place; I remember it now. Help me out, Mr. Melville; these country winds have quite starched my limbs, and I'm stiff as your cravat."

"My Lel, I do verily believe!" cried the Colonel, rushing to meet her as she leaped lightly from the sleigh. "Lel, Lel, is not this you?"

"All that's left of me, uncle, and this is my very good friend, Mr. George Melville, a young gentleman who can catch a trout, shoot a partridge, play all fours, and sing divinely. Take care how you hug me, uncle; I'm cold as an icicle; you'll break my bones; wait till I get warm," and, disengaging herself, she ran into the parlor and threw herself on her knees before the fire.

Mrs. Cleveland rose in amazement at this abrupt entry, and Ellen, enjoying her surprise, took off her bonnet, threw back her long golden curls, and still kneeling and laughing, said : —

"Now, Aunt Mary, take a good long look, don't you know me?"

"Ellen Almy!" exclaimed Mrs. Cleveland, embracing her, as the Colonel entered, followed by Agnes and George Melville.

Without a word, Ellen flew towards Agnes, and, seizing her by the hand, led her as close to the lamp on the table as she could get. There she stood, eyeing her from head to foot, so comically that Agnes could not keep from smiling.

"So this is my little cousin with whom I played, and quarreled, and made up, ten years ago! Do you remember me, Agnes?" And the expression of her bright face suddenly changed, her eyes filled with tears, and she threw her arms around her cousin's neck.

"They told me," she continued, raising her head from her friend's shoulder, "that you had grown up to be a sweet creature, with black hair, black eyes, rosy cheeks, and cherry lips, but I little expected to find such an absolute beauty."

"Come Ellen, no flattery here," interposed Mrs. Cleveland. Ellen, with a look of mock gravity and displeasure, walked slowly up to her aunt, and looking reproachfully into her eyes, replied : —

"Madam, you do me great injustice; in the first place, my name is Lel, not Ellen. The world is full of Ellens, but there's only one Lel, isn't there, uncle? Secondly, though my faults are as innumerable as your virtues, I have not to answer for the sin of saying what I do not think."

"But what we think is often flattery," replied her aunt.

"Then, to please you, I'll stop saying what I think;" and laughing more merrily than ever, she sprang upon the Colonel, saying, "Now that I'm thawed you may hug me as much as you please;" and the old gentleman took her at her word.

There was silence for a moment. Ellen, of course, was the first one to break it, —

"My goodness, Mr. Melville, excuse me; but indeed I forgot all about you; have you been in the room all this time? Permit me, sir; Ag, my friend, Mr. Melville, sweet name, isn't it? Mr. Melville, my cousin, Miss Agnes Cleveland, just from school, as that blush demonstrates. I wish *I* could blush!"

Even Mrs. Cleveland laughed at this, and before she had ceased Charley appeared, and with his best bow announced supper.

Ellen sat next to Agnes. "Oh, Aggie," she said, "I feel so happy! Do you remember the long walk we took one first of May, the day I fell in the creek and scared off uncle's trout for a week? Do you remember the talk we had, whilst I sat on the grass drying off in the sun?"

A smile played over Agnes's face as she answered, "I have not forgotten anything, Ellen"——

' " *Lel!* I tell you!" cried her cousin. "You know we were talking about the future that morning, and you said you'd marry a soldier, and I"——

"Determined to have a circus rider."

"That his neck might be broken as speedily as possible," suggested Melville.

Lel eyed him meaningly across the table and said, "Exactly! Aunt Mary, this is the same milk-toast 'you used to give us; where's the honey?"

Charley brought it.

When the brief meal was over Agnes and her cousin, arm-in-arm, led the way to the parlor.

"Put your hand on the table, Ag; there; yours is larger than mine, but it's whiter too. Now, take off your shoe; what! your foot smaller than mine! I don't believe it. Let's see — mercy! Were you ever in China?"

"Flattering again?" said Mrs. Cleveland.

"By no means," answered Ellen, "I was alluding to her teeth.

> ' In China none hold women sweet,
> Unless their snags are black as jet.'

as old Prior says;" and she pointed (Agnes was laughing) to the ivory gleaming between her lips.

"Lel" said the Colonel, from his arm-chair, "under what impulse, or by what accident, did you blunder on us, after a meditated, deliberate, and most unpardonable absence of nearly ten years?"

"After excusing myself from the accusation, I'll answer the rest of the question. I was eight years old when I left here; five years were lost at boarding-school; two more wasted at a preparatory academy for fashionable life. Of course you could not expect me to interrupt my education merely to see you. Father wouldn't listen to it. Then I was packed off to Europe for two years, to obtain a fine classical finish, and on my return there were so many entertainments that for two seasons I had not a moment to spare my relatives and friends, without doing injustice to my multitudinous admirers. Isn't it so, Mr. Melville?"

Melville drew a long breath, and answered "Yes."

"Agnes, that was meant for a sigh," resumed the lively girl; "he is incorrigibly romantic. Well, uncle, one morning I found myself not fifty miles from here, on a wedding frolic, and as the sleighing was good it struck me to comfort your old eyes by my presence, especially as there is a chance of the snow's melting and a ride

back in the mud.   Where shall we go to-night,
Aggie?"

"To bed, I suppose," said Agnes, after seeing
the drift of the question.

"Do you go to bed every night, Agnes?"

"Yes."

"But before that?   Oh, dear!   Is there nothing to be seen about here? no sights, no rustic
soirees, no opera?   How do you manage to exist
between nine and twelve?"

"By talking and sleeping."

"No sleeping now," observed Melville, *sotto
voce*, to the Colonel.

"A piano, as I live," went on Lel, disregarding
the allusion to her loquacity, "strike a note and
I'm dumb.   Come, Agnes, let me see how you've
been taught."

Agnes at once consented and played a theme
with variations by Hertz.   Lel was silent, according to promise; but hardly had the last note
sounded, than she broke forth : —

"Cousin, do you call that playing?   Listen to
me!"   She sat down to the instrument, and,
after a short prelude, began an adagio of Beethoven's.   During the first bar her face changed;
as she went on her eye seemed to catch the
inspiration of the music; the giddy, laughing girl
fled before something nobler; she was another

being. Agnes stood almost breathless beside her, surveying her cousin in joy and wonder. As the sublime melody rolled on, gathering strength from the deepening harmony, her tears started ; and when the piece was over, unable to restrain the impulse, she clasped Lel in her arms. She was too good, too pure, not to perceive her own inferiority, and rejoice in it.

"My dear Lel," she said, " you have given me a lesson I shall never forget ! "

" Imitate me in everything, cousin, and you will be perfect," said Lel.

Melville, whom the adagio had visibly affected, advanced to the piano.

"Miss Almy," he said, "play that again, and I'm yours forever."

Lel looked at him until he laughed in spite of himself, and then, without discontinuing her gaze, began to sing *John Anderson, my Joe John,* whilst Melville retreated in dismay. The conversation soon became general, and thus passed Lel's first evening at Loretto.

CHAPTER III.

TWO new pieces are now in motion at Loretto — Ellen Almy and George Melville. In a few words, perhaps, we may bring them nearer to the eye.

Lel, let us call her so, for it is a sweet name either in itself or from association, was a year younger than Agnes. The daughter of a wealthy merchant, with all the advantages of wealth and fashion, gifted with no ordinary share of personal beauty, and peculiarly endowed with that indescribable fascination of manner which has no name, Lel was a pet wherever she went. She was above envy and without a rival. Whatever she did became a law for the satellites around her; scarcely had a new fancy struck her before it was reduced to practice, and once realized it grew into a fashion. Her actions and sayings were retailed at second-hand, and sought after with much avidity by all those who borrow from the fruitfulness of others to supply their own mental sterility.

Of course Lel had been spoiled. Most persons only knew her as a light-hearted, flippant girl, with wit enough to amuse others, but without prudence to govern herself. But those who looked beneath the transparent surface could see a noble vein of deep feeling, responding firmly and healthfully to every genuine touch. Lel had much talent and more genius; she acquired without much difficulty what others had written, but rose without an effort to higher things, of which they never dreamed. There are many in the world who resemble her; many we meet daily in the morning and in the evening, who to the same levity unite a certain strength and elevation of character; but there are few who equal her, few who combine such girlish merriment with such womanly worth.

Lel's mother had been a Catholic, but she was dead, and her father, being a Protestant, gave her a Protestant Episcopalian education. Of Catholics she knew little save from stereotype calumny, and from her own juvenile observations in France, Spain, and Italy.

George Melville was near thirty. Early in life he was left lord of himself, sole heir to a large fortune. There was nothing remarkable in his person beside a high forehead and a bright eye; but all his friends considered him attractive. There was more in him than was seen at first, much that was only perceptible to the few who knew him well. He had been a hard student all his life, and gave to the classics the long winter evenings so generally sacred to revelry and dissipation. He did not, however, totally abstain from society, but carefully avoided becoming its slave. To strangers he was reserved and formal, with others cheerful and familiar. There was an air of close scrutiny about him from which ninety-nine in a hundred shrank. Lel was not one of these; she defied both competition and scrutiny. She and Melville, though apparently diametrically opposite in taste and disposition, had been fast friends for more than a year, and it was rumored that they were engaged to be married. This was false, however, not one word of love having passed between them. The masses, the unreflecting and unfeeling list of visitors, wondered at their intimacy; though surely it was not surprising that Melville should discover Lel's real value, or that she should prefer his intellectual gifts to the superficial endowments of the bulk of her acquaintances.

"Charley!" cried the Colonel, the next morning, after breakfast, "saddle Fleetly for Mr. Melville, and Lilly for Miss Agnes! Do you hear, my boy? Off with you, and bring them up in five minutes. Mind the girths, you rascal, there are two precious lives depending on the proper hole in a leather strap."

"And you don't mean to order a horse for

me," muttered Lel, pouting as she spoke; "am I to remain here for your special edification?"

"You must not begrudge me an hour this morning," answered her uncle. "I will introduce you to the farm, my dear child, and counteract your excessive affectation by an infusion of rusticity."

"Well," replied Lel, as Charley and the horses appeared, "I shall endèavor to profit by the manners of your turkeys, chickens, pigeons, pigs, cows; and I doubt not, but that after a diligent study of your sheep, I shall prove an absolute lamb. Farewell, *mes amis!*" she exclaimed, as Agnes and Melville mounted. "Farewell!" she repeated, as they galloped off, and turning to her uncle, looked him steadily and seriously in the face.

Mrs. Cleveland was sewing in the back parlor. A peculiarly sly expression played around the corners of the Colonel's mouth, and he glanced stealthily towards the back parlor.

"Now," Lel, he said, with great significance, "come to my sanctum, and I'll show you my tackle."

The Colonel's *Sanctum* was a small room next his chamber. It contained all his sporting apparatus, all his curiosities, all his petty bachelor contrivances, a large bookcase crowded with Turf Registers and Treatises on Angling, heaped over noble editions of the English essayists and the old English dramatists. A round table stood in the centre, covered with papers, heaped up in that glorious confusion which an author loves and a housekeeper hates. Two rocking-chairs and a red lounge were the only seats.

Lel took one chair, the Colonel the other.

"Oh, uncle," said Lel, shaking her finger at him, "what a little lying hypocrite you have made me."

"In a good cause, my queen," replied the old man.

"You wrote me word that Agnes intended to bury her beauty in a convent, and that I must come and prevent it. But what possessed you to insist on my dropping in as if by accident, with a lie on my lips? Oh, it kills me to play the hypocrite! I was tempted, in spite of your commands, to salute Agnes by falling on her neck, and declaring that if she ever took the veil it would have to go over my head too, all the priests in Christendom to the contrary notwithstanding."

"Ha! ha!" laughed the Colonel; "very good, very good, my own sweet pet. But mark me, Lel, if her mother suspects us we are gone.

I tell you that Agnes Cleveland, in her cradle, was devoted to the cloister; and I know my sister well enough to assert that if we show our hand we lose the stake."

"Very well, uncle, as you say. Oh, Lel, Lel, have you come to this! a snake in the grass — a wily, subtle, deep designing serpent. What would Melville say?"

"Whatever he pleases," interposed the Colonel haughtily. "Listen, Lel, my plan is briefly this: while you stay, to consecrate all your energy, all your fascination, all your genius, to divert your cousin's mind from her present purpose, and spread out before her all the allurements of refined society. But do it gradually, smoothly, gently; do it so that the transition will be unfelt, so that her mother" ——

"Will have every reason to despise me!" cried Lel, springing to her feet. "Yet, it must be done! The life I lead is bad enough, God knows, but it's better than a convent."

Lel said this mournfully. She was standing by the window, her hand resting on a magnificent pair of antlers, whose ample arms sustained a powder-flask, shot-pouch, bird-bag, and quite a variety of old hats and caps adapted to all the seasons and every species of weather. The Colonel sat silently eyeing her, as if not a little puzzled.

Lel looked out upon the snow-clad plain, upon the pale blue wintry sky, and fell into a revery, that strange compound of thought and feeling which soothes and saddens too. She was startled from it by a heavy hand on her shoulder. She turned; the Colonel stood beside her; his cheeks were wet with tears, his upper lip was quivering.

"Lel," he said, "if what I ask is painful, I will not demand it; but" — the words died away in his throat.

Lel dried his eyes and her own with her handkerchief. "Uncle!" she exclaimed, impetuously, the road to heaven is not by trampling on your heart, and Agnes must take another path! Your hand, uncle!" They joined hands. "I solemnly pledge myself to wean Agnes from her choice of a religious life, if all the influence at my command can do it! I will tell her the story that enchanted me; I will reveal the beautiful visions that seemed to hover before me; I will tell her of the raptures I have had and of the raptures I still expect. If she resists me she's invincible!"

"Bless you! bless you, Lel!" repeated the Colonel, putting back her hair, and pressing her head to his bosom. Though for ten years he had rarely seen her, and then only for a day or two as he travelled, yet, at that moment, she was almost as dear to him as Agnes. "You have given me new life, my child; there's victory in your flashing face! Can you guess my next great move?"

"Take Agnes home with me after Christmas?"

"Eh? Have you fathomed your old uncle so soon? To be sure; go with you she must! Take her to every opera and every ball " ——

"No, no," broke in Lel; " I shall carefully select from both, or you'll soon have her here by telegraph, more eager than ever for the convent."

" Introduce her to the handsomest men "——

" And disgust her at once."

"Surround her with stylish women " ——

" And sicken her completely."

" Well, then," suggested the Colonel, taken sadly aback, " begin by accustoming her to small tea-parties where intelligence makes the absence of music and dancing unfelt."

Lel fairly screamed and laughed till she reeled back again to the window.

"Take her to a tea-party! My dear, good-for-nothing old uncle, why you'd have us *both* back for the convent!"

"Lel,' said the Colonel, and stopped short. Lel turned, expecting something else; her bright eyes glittering from laughter, like violets, dewy in the morning.

"Lel"— He looked, up and catching her mischievous glance, inwardly admitted that he was only making himself ridiculous, and turning away to save his dignity, added, "Do just as you please, and be hanged to you!"

"Tell me, uncle, and tell me truly, am I not the abler tactician on my own ground? Your conception of the game is a masterpiece, but leave the details to me."

"Right, right, you're always right."

"I knew a young girl, situated just as Agnes is, who became a nun because her friends over-did it in trying to prevent her. I don't often praise myself, but I can manage the human heart as easily as I can a horse, provided I once get the reins."

"We must not let her mother suspect; be prudent, Lel."

Lel was looking out of the window, instead of listening.

"What fine buildings are those? she asked."

"The convent," replied the Colonel, suppress-ing a curse.

"The convent!" said Lel, musing. "So it is, there's the old house; but there are so many new ones around it, it's not easily seen. Ah me! I don't wonder Ag wants to stay there. Nonsense! they'd cut off all her beautiful black hair, and crimp her face up in a skull-cap, and set her to scrubbing floors and scouring pots. She *shan't* go!"

"She *shan't!*" responded the Colonel, "and now, my sister, I cry, *check!*"

Thus plotted Lel and the Colonel, whilst Agnes, little suspecting what mischief they were hatching, rode gayly beside George Melville. Melville was much interested in his companion. She was a new character to him; new, not only because the inexperienced school-girl peeped from almost every sentence, or because her manners were artless and unvarnished by social attrition, though affable, striking, and dignified by interior correctness and feeling; Melville had seen many such. It may have been this, in part, but there was something else, something entirely new, yet still suggesting things which had passed for him, but which might come again; something admired without knowing why; something which repelled while it attracted.

The world has some redeeming points, and society might be worse: public opinion is yet sufficiently Christian to discountenance open crime. The thousands we meet have nothing to blush for; their names are stainless, their eyes are bright and fearless, their hopes are high, there is no brand on the brow; the tribunal to which they appeal acquits and commends; their belief in their own integrity, like a good conscience, makes them lovely and enchanting. But when God and not man affixes the seal of innocence, when the soul, pure in thought as well as in act, walks in the midst of "a thousand liveried angels," how different, how different! Melville was a man of strong sense and true feeling, a keen, experienced observer, a tourist of more than half the world; but he found Agnes a new character, one he had yet to read.

At first he found it difficult to remove her embarrassment and to converse as cordially as he wished. But the sun was bright, and the horses bounded along; long before their return, Melville had conquered the difficulty, and even reached that desirable point, seldom soon, and sometimes never gained, where people exchange thoughts as well as words.

"Aggie, dear," said Lel, as they alighted, "do you know that you're just one-half hour after dinner time?"

CHAPTER IV.

HE scene is still the same; but patience, reader, it will soon be changed. There are not many spots, even in your fancy, superior to Loretto, poorly as our meagre description reflects its beauty. We might labor for hours to picture all its charms, to copy the fine prospect it commanded, without making it a whit more enchanting. Loretto had no water-falls around it, no gloomy, splendid glens, no towering masses of rock, cleaving the clouds in stern sublimity; but every tree, every field, every outline of the undulating plain had a meaning; the place had a Genius, the indefinable spirit of beauty haunted the spot.

Let us spend a few more evenings there: they will not be lost; they are necessary to the sequel. Let us still linger around that bright, crackling, intelligent wood-fire, inspiriting that plain little parlor, before we are transported by Lel's magic to the coal furnaces and sumptuous drawing-rooms of the city. Christmas is but two days off, and then we leave, not to return till the forest trees are in leaf, the orchards heavy with fruit; not to return until the spring flowers have passed away and the busy bees have exhausted the honeysuckles wreathing the white porches of Loretto.

"Why are you so sad, Lel?" said Mrs. Cleveland.

"Because I am going to leave you to-morrow."

"To-morrow!" echoed Agnes.

"To-morrow!" repeated the Colonel.

"I must," said Lel, "or father will have all the alarm bells in town ringing for me, and all the constables in creation after Mr. Melville."

"Are you tired of our solitude?" asked her aunt.

"No, aunt; but I am sure Mr. Melville is heartily sick of your country monotony, and longs for the variable gayety he has made essential to his existence. Much as I wish to stay I am not selfish enough to enjoy myself at his expense."

"Is that your only reason?" said Melville.

"Not the only one, but still a sufficient one for a creature as considerative and self-sacrificing as I."

"Lel!" gasped the Colonel, thumping the floor with his stick, "are you serious?"

'"As serious as I ever was, or ever expect to be."

"Do you love me, Lel?"

"Yes."

"Then stay."

"Can't, uncle."

"Look'ee, my young girl, I am not used to contradiction."

"Nor I either," retorted Lel.

"Do you dare to follow your inclinations in spite of my commands?"

"Dare you pretend to command my inclinations? No man in Christendom can boast of that. Leaving Agnes is the hardest part of it. If only you and Aunt Mary were in the case, I might get up a parting tear; but it would dry before it reached my mouth."

"I assure you, Miss Almy," said Melville, "that so far from wishing to go"——

"Did you think me in earnest when I spoke of you?" replied Lel. "Oh, George Melville! George Melville! the cottage of Loretto is the tomb of your wit!"

"Lel!" said Agnes, taking her hand and kneeling down before her, "Lel, I have been silent, because I did not believe you, because I don't, can't, and won't believe you. Meet me now with your wild, wicked blue eyes, and tell if you will not spend Christmas with us."

Lel hesitated some seconds, and then replied:—

"On one condition, Agnes, I will."

"Name it! name it! cried the Colonel, brightening like snow in the morning. "We grant it in advance."

"That you accompany me home, Agnes," said Lel, leaning forward, and for the first time looking her cousin full in the face. There was an earnestness in Lel's manner that could not be misinterpreted, and Agnes, taken by surprise, continued to gaze at her, not a little bewildered by the proposition. It was not long, however, before her eye wandered to her mother. Lel saw the glance, and dreading it, rose quick as lightning, and throwing her arms around Mrs. Cleveland's neck, exclaimed, —

"My dearest aunt, if you deny me this, we part forever. Never again shall Lel's foot cross this time-honored threshhold, never again shall your toast and honey bless my lips, never again shall these arms, which a statue might envy, be your necklace! I will never play for you, never sing for you, never dance for you, and, what is more, I'll never pray for you. Still stern and unrelenting? Oh, Aunt Mary, we will guard her as the apple of our eye; we'll have two dragons in special attendance; the wind shall be tempered to suit her; society decimated to please her, and, listen, Aunt Mary, the rose shall bloom brighter in her cheeks, her form shall be fuller

and her step freer; and you shall have her back
again, the same noble, beautiful, peerless Agnes!"

"This is all so sudden," said Mrs. Cleveland,
"that I cannot possibly give you an answer
to-night."

"Give me an answer to-morrow, and remember
my threats! they are not to be disregarded.
And as for. you, my veteran," continued Lel,
leaping upon the Colonel, if you do not use all
your authority in my favor I'll never call you
uncle again!"

"Can't spare Aggie!" muttered the Colonel,
afraid to look up lest his face should betray his
thoughts.

"Better spare her a month, Colonel, than lose
her forever;" and she brought her face close to
his.

"God bless you!" he whispered in her ear.

"God forgive me!" she said in her heart; and
adding aloud—"I will return in a moment,"
left the room laughing.

She went to her chamber, groping her way in
the dark and blinded by her tears. She knelt in
the clear moonlight at the foot of her bed.

"Oh, God!" she said—for in moments of
anguish we often think aloud—"can I lead this
young angel forth from this holy solitude to

share with me the spurious honors, the tinsel trappings I covet and despise? Shall I infect her with the fatal thirst for admiration and excitement which consumes me? I *will* not!" She started to her feet. "And yet — and yet — to wither in a convent — to drag out life, the miserable dupe of suicidal superstition. Could I stand by and see the fillets put on her neck as the black-robed executioner leads her to the shambles? No, Agnes, you shall *try* the world, at least. If it does not sicken you, I think there is more of the nun in me than in you!"

She leaned out of the window until the cold night air dried her tears; then carefully washed her eyes and returned to the parlor.

"Come, Ag, a truce to thought, it's a bad companion. Don't sit there like a maid of marble, come closer to me. Uncle, let your stick alone, I don't want a drum *obligato.* Don't breathe so hard, Mr. Melville."

With this, Lel began the following song, as merrily as if she had not wept since childhood: —

"There was a time when she rose to greet me.
  But what, alas, cared I !
For well I knew she flew to meet me,
  Yet met me with a sigh.

I left her in her deep dejection,
  And laughed with merry men.
What cared I for her true affection —
  I did not love her then!

But now I wander weak and weary,
  And what, alas, cares she!
I lost her love, and life grew dreary —
  She scarce remembers me!
In vain, in vain I now implore her,
  She spurns my tearful vow:
Too late, too late, I now adore her —
  She does not love me now!"

As Lel concluded, she turned to Melville. She had sung with even more point than the words seemed to suggest — and the look she gave Melville meant something, too, whatever it was.

"I never heard that before," said Melville, from his seat.

"You'll hear it again though," said Lel.

"Who's the composer?" he asked.

"Words and music perpetrated by your humble servant. Now, sir, as the groves of Loretto are not yet honeyed by your voice, I abdicate in your favor. Agnes, ask him to sing '*I am a Wanderer;*' it is a wild, diabolical thing, and he delights in it."

Melville, thus appealed to, did not wait for Agnes to ask him.

"Begin, begin!" cried Lel, seating herself beside Mrs. Cleveland. "Let your articulation be "— She bit her lip and crossed her arms meekly over her breast. Melville was singing: —

> " I am a wanderer!
>   Far from home, far from her —
>   The lady whom I left in tears,
>   Whose tears still flow for me,
>   The bride I have not seen for years,
>   And never more may see !
>
> " Houseless and penniless,
>   None to love, none to bless !
>   Oh! wronged and wronging, let me rave —
>   In death our tears are dried;
>   I'll sleep as soundly in the grave
>   As ever at her side !"

The wild ballad was followed by a dead silence; even Lel was hushed. Agnes was startled; the Colonel looked anxiously at Mrs. Cleveland, whose face was supported and concealed by her hand. To Melville, the long pause was painful, his powerful voice and the almost unearthly music had produced an effect greater than he designed or wished.

" A strange song, that, Colonel Cleverton," he said, striking some chords carelessly; "and it came into my possession in a very singular way.

I was reading a new overture of Mendelssohn's, at a music store at London, when my attention was diverted by a conversation between the proprietor and a middle-aged gentleman who had entered. I could not remove my eyes from the stranger — he fascinated me. His dress was negligent, his coat old and faded, but his bearing proud and graceful. I cannot describe his head and face — you may have seen the same expression in a sculptor's ideal of manly power and beauty. It seemed as if disappointment or remorse had frozen from it every particle of joy; but there was left a reckless disdain of everything human or superhuman, and the shadow of a great mind embittered by adversity and enfeebled by dissipation."

Had Melville looked towards the corner where Mrs. Cleveland sat he would have paused; but observing that Agnes was listening intently he continued, —

"He came to sell the song. As the publisher was courteously returning it, I asked permission to glance at it. He assented coldly and with a smile of scorn almost insulting. The daring originality of every phrase — the wild tide of melody made me stare in astonishment at the stranger who claimed to be the author. The same withering smile was on his face. We were standing beside a piano, and, without more ado, I sang it with all the feeling inspired by the novelty of the music and the man. It was my turn of triumph then. Before I had well finished the stranger seized my hand—his thin cheeks flushed and a mist gathered in his eyes.

" '*You* understand me,' he said.

" ' Will you sell me this song?' I asked.

"The flush in his cheek deepened as he replied : —

" 'Are you not an American?'

" "I bowed.

" 'Do you return to your country?'

" ' Yes.'

" 'Then honor me by accepting my song.'

" He saluted me cordially, and brushing quickly by the publisher, would have gone without another word. Unwilling to part from him thus I caught him by the arm.

" 'May I ask your name?' I said.

" 'I have none.'

" ' Stay, sir, I beg you, and let us enjoy one hour of music together.'

" ' I no longer *enjoy* music,' he replied, with an accent that made me shudder.

"I gave him my card, saying, 'Pray, let us meet again.'

" 'In heaven, perhaps,' was the only answer;

and he stepped into the street, leaving me rooted to the floor in amazement. He remains a mystery to this day: I can see him now — the deep scar on his forehead " —

As if her heart had burst, a deep groan came from Mrs. Cleveland's breast.

" Death and madness ! " muttered the Colonel, tottering toward her; but Agnes anticipated him.

" It is nothing, Agnes," whispered Mrs. Cleveland, recovering herself. " It will pass off in an instant, only a momentary faintness. A glass of water, my child ! "

The cloud on the Colonel's brow was terrible.

" Could you not see," said Lel, aside to Melville, " that every word you uttered was a dagger plunged into that woman's heart ! "

" More mystery, more mystery," said Melville. " What have I done ? "

" God knows ! But never sing that song again."

CHAPTER V.

A S Charley was covering up the parlor fire for the night Agnes left Lel and went to her mother's chamber. She had never heard her father's name mentioned;

she rarely thought of a father, and whenever she did it was only to offer up a fervent prayer for one who had died before she was old enough to know or to love him. But Melville's song, her uncle's frown, and her mother's anguish had revealed a secret hitherto unsuspected; her memory darted, like a ray of light, farther back into her life, and it seemed to her that she had loved another before she loved the Colonel, one who was all kindness, one who sang to her before she came to Loretto, one who was with her day and night, one whom she suddenly missed and wept for. Was it her father, and was he alive? Unable to answer, unable to satisfy or control her thousand vague conjectures, she now sought her mother to escape the torture of doubt. Agnes had seen little of the world; her observation had been limited to Loretto and the adjacent village; but her inexperience was amply supplied by that keen, quick insight which needs not the lamp of time or trial to read the book of human nature. Before Melville had concluded his narrative she suspected; when the deep groan interrupted him, she knew the truth.

Mrs. Cleveland rose from her knees as Agnes entered, and they sat down together on the bed. The first look revealed their thoughts, and they

embraced in silence. Much as Agnes wished to
speak it was long before her working lips could
pronounce the question she wished yet feared
to utter. At last, firmly and rapidly, the question came, —

" Is my father living ? "

A flood of tears was the only reply; for the
full heart must overflow before it speaks. But
Mrs. Cleveland had trained herself to resignation in the school of the cross; the unspoken
prayer sped from her uplifted eye, and stilled
her breast, and calmed her throbbing heart, and
poured light and sweetness over the waters of
bitterness on her face. Agnes waited till all was
calm, and then repeated more firmly and distinctly still —

" Is my father living ? "

" I know not ! "

She had controlled her emotion until then, —
that fair young girl — she had nerved herself to
hear, unshrinking, whether he was alive or dead,
but she was unprepared for this terrible announce-
ment ; unprepared to remain longer in suspense ;
unprepared to hear from her mother's lips this
fearful ignorance of her father's fate. The dark
wavering line of sudden agony rose in her forehead, and she clasped her hands in supplication
and terror ; pale and motionless as death she sat,

her eyes fixed on her mother's, crouching as though she shrank from another word.

"I can tell you nothing more, my child," Mrs. Cleveland said, employing as she spoke all the arts of maternal love to heal the wound she had inflicted; "I can tell you nothing more. Trust to God and pray for your father. We may meet again, if not here, in heaven!"

Ay, to those who live for this world with scarce a thought of the next, who centre all their hopes, fears, joys, sorrows, thoughts, passions *here*, who look on death as the end of all, who know God only by reputation, who trust not his mercy in misfortune and ask not his blessing in prosperity, who in health or sickness fly to man as the sole companion, the sole comforter, — to these, indeed, *a meeting in heaven* means nothing; but to those who look beyond the grave for their true home, who hail death as the end of exile, the beginning of life, who hold the accidents of time light in comparison with their lot in eternity, who stake not their happiness on human calculation, who exult when the world cries "Despair!" who, amid change, and storm, and light, and darkness, preserve a correspondence fixed above; who, though in daily contact with man, are in constant communion with God, living to love in bliss hereafter, to these *a meet-*

ing in heaven is an appreciable promise, a blessing that takes the sting from parting; and they know not how to say "Farewell forever!"

Years of consolation could not have imparted to Agnes the exquisite relief of that one word. "Yes, in heaven!" she said, again and again, and knelt with her mother almost rejoicing.

When Mrs. Cleveland was alone her mind gradually wandered from the painful subject which had engrossed it to the consideration of Lel's proposition. She had never parted from Agnes except to place her at the convent school, where all was harmony and peace, where the licensed pride and revelry of society found no footing. She mistrusted the influence of fashionable life on any pure, young heart; she was happy in her daughter's choice; she did not believe that temptation must be sought and vanquished before a decision is made. But she feared precipitation, she feared lest the strict seclusion in which Agnes had been brought up might have misled her by making habit seem vocation. She thought it better that her daughter should see something of the world before she renounced it. She was not conscious of one spark of pride in her daughter's beauty, or of ambition to see it triumph in the arena of fashion. She regarded marriage as a very questionable blessing, and certainly aspired not to any brilliant alliance. But Mrs. Cleveland was a woman and a mother; she did not fully consider the danger of gazing on the pomp and splendor and magic in which the arch-demon steeps and gilds the orgies of his votaries; it did not strike her that there was not the least occasion to witness or bid adieu to the pleasures Agnes could never share. She did not like to judge the world too harshly; there were many pure, pious people in it, who lived, as she did, apart from its excesses and in the enjoyment of its comforts; there were some who glided uncontaminated through all its dangerous mazes, guided by one faithful thread that brought them safely out. Lel was wild and light, but truehearted and sensible withal; a fortnight or a month could make no change in Agnes, unless such were the will of God. But Mrs. Cleveland came to no conclusion of her own, except to leave the matter with Agnes and her confessor. Upon this delicate and all important point her own reasoning failed to satisfy her; she felt that she needed advice in a question so dear to her, advice from those who were commissioned to instruct. Her humility was equal to her firmness; for her firmness proceeded not from self-reliance, but from reliance on God.

Agnes, younger in grief than her mother, remained awake long after the latter slept, thinking of her father and watching Lel, who was slumbering so calmly beside her. With Agnes it was a night of almost ceaseless prayer, — of prayer more refreshing then than sleep. Presently the taper grew pale in the dawn, and the merry sunbeams tipped the window curtains with gold — the domestics were astir — it was the morning of Christmas eve.

"Now," cried Lel, "for another day at Loretto!"

"I knew you did not mean to leave me," said Agnes.

Lel drew back abashed, as she recollected her imperious declaration of last night, and some moments elapsed before she added, with the arch gravity she could so well assume, —

"*Provided*, Ag! provided, I can thus purchase leave of absence for you."

But the saving clause came too late. A word, a look, a blush, a pause, may defeat the subtlest schemes, even when nearly perfected; just as the snapping of a twig betrays and foils the ambushed hunter when surest of his prey. Agnes remembered now some strange looks that had passed between Lel and the Colonel, — she remembered many of Lel's remarks, which implied a knowledge of her determination to embrace a religious life, — and, after a rapid review of all that had lately happened, she felt sure that Lel had not come to Loretto without a purpose or uninvited.

Lel, confident that she had parried suspicion, ascribed the evident tumult in her cousin's mind to Melville's song and the subsequent interview with her mother. Lel had heard her father allude vaguely to Mrs. Cleveland's misfortune, and guessed the nature of it. "Poor girl," she murmured inaudibly, "no wonder she is so thoughtful!"

For once in her life Lel was deceived. We have already indicated the process by which Agnes discovered, or thought she had discovered, a deliberate, premeditated plan; but she did not stop there. She loved Lel as she stood there before her, young, gifted, beautiful; the few days they had spent together had sufficed to endear them mutually to each other; like two sweet springs, they met and then flowed on together. Agnes required no assistance in detecting her cousin's virtues, no monitor to point out her imperfections. She knew her as if by inspiration. Agnes was not thinking of her father, but of her who stood before her, young, gifted, beautiful. A heroic purpose crossed her mind, the ardor of a missionary glowed in her cheeks, and if mortals are ever commissioned to aid an angel guardian Agnes felt the call. Without presumption, but in hope and joy, she silently folded Lel to her heart, vowing, —

" *You came to change me; I go to change you!* "

Lel, at a loss to account for so much emotion and so little grief, could not help saying, with a smile, —

" Ag, I know you're unhappy, and yet you're not sad. Does Catholic sorrow differ from Protestant sorrow ? "

" It may, perhaps; I know too little of your heresy to decide."

" Then how do you know it's a heresy ? " suggested Lel, quickly and maliciously.

" Because the church brands it heresy. *I* am not the judge."

" Oh, Aggie, Aggie, how delightfully humble your church is ! "

" Humbler, though infallible, than you erring and culpable individuals who presume to judge her."

This was the first time, and then accidentally, that the two friends touched controversy ; they had no relish for it. But having once crossed weapons playfully, the contest might have waxed warmer had not the Colonel's sonorous voice, echoing up the stairs, terminated the battle thus: "Girls, are you ever coming down to breakfast?"

We need not tell how Lel redoubled her entreaties, how Melville delicately aided her to induce Mrs. Cleveland to consent at once to a brief separation from her daughter, or how the Colonel threw all the influence of authoritative silence in Lel's favor, saying nothing on either side, but expressing by every limb, feature, motion — "Let her go!"

"I will decide to-night," was Mrs. Cleveland's only answer to every appeal.

In the afternoon, Agnes and her mother ordered Charley to get ready their snug country wagon for the convent.

"Lel," said Agnes, as she was stepping into the carriage, "the Litany will be sung at six, and I want you to hear it. You and Mr. Melville can leave here at five and be in time."

"Gone to consult her confessor," muttered the Colonel, as Charley flourished his whip; "he will never let her go."

"Then," returned Lel, "there's but one thing left — Mr. Melville must challenge him."

The Colonel was in no laughing humor. He did his best to content himself in the cottage, exhausting every position possible to the human body, and exploring every room. in the house, without satisfaction or repose. Finally, he caught up his gun and swore he would have a brace of partridges for supper.

Lel and Melville were left alone without exactly knowing what to do. A shade passed over the young girl's brow as she watched Melville intently for a while, as he sat abstractedly gazing toward the convent. But her glad, gay look soon returned, and she said, —

"I wonder whether a little music will not keep us alive until five o'clock."

For some minutes she played without an aim, trifling with some pretty melodies that came first into her mind; but presently higher thoughts began to dawn, and she blended into one superb whole a thousand fragments of fine ideas, some original, some remembered, until Melville himself, often as he had witnessed these flights of genius, was fairly astounded. The cottage seemed to be alive with music, as Lel, forgetful of herself, of him, and of all else, save the beauty she was creating, lovelier than she had ever been, poured forth the unpremeditated strain. The movement was rapid but sad, though variable as an April morning, until there seemed to be an evident concentration of one idea; and then, gathering all her strength for the sublime theme, which she had been almost imperceptibly approaching, she dashed without pause or breathing into a figure of John Sebastian Bach's. Every touch unfolded some exquisite passage in the master's life, and Melville could see the fair-haired child of genius studying thorough-bass by moonlight, lest his jealous brother, catching the gleam of his lamp, should send him to the garret. He could see him toiling on cheerfully through persecution and neglect, until in the full blaze of acknowledged superiority he rose like the day-star from the mists of the horizon.

"What do you think of that?" cried Lel, as evidently delighted as though another had performed, with tears still in her eyes.

"I wish it had lasted forever," was Melville's enthusiastic reply.

CHAPTER VI.

IT was quite dark when Lel and Melville entered the convent chapel. Lel was admitted, at Mrs. Cleveland's instance, through the private door. The tapers on the altar were not yet lit, and the soft light of a single lamp produced an effect more solemn than darkness. A novice showed her to a pew, where she sat down in silence, well pleased to have some moments for reflection in a place so favorable to meditation.

Melville was conducted to a recess on the right of the altar. He looked anxiously round for Agnes and her mother, but they were either invisible or absent. Had the folding doors of the sacristy been open he would have seen the confessor of the convent sitting between Mrs. Cleveland and Agnes, and had he been a little nearer, might have heard the end of a discussion in which he was interested even more deeply than he imagined.

The confessor was a middle-aged man, tall and spare, slightly bald, his face marked with that beautiful character of meekness and benevolence which belongs to those alone who ever feel that the eye of God is on them. A life of piety and self-denial is marked by lines as legible as the furrows which irreligion and profligacy plough; there needed not the surplice and the cassock to point him out as "a man of God."

Mrs. Cleveland and Agnes, after receiving absolution, had called him into the sacristy and acquainted him with Lel's proposition.

"I am somewhat afraid of this same Lel," he said, after they had sketched her character. "I should not like to trust our rustic little Agnes with so accomplished a belle. Do you think it advisable, madam?"

"I leave the matter entirely with you," Mrs. Cleveland replied.

"And what says Agnes?"

"I wish to go," returned Agnes, grasping his hand.

"You wish to go!" repeated the confessor, earnestly surveying his youthful charge, his voice faltering as he spoke, in astonishment and fear.

"Yes," cried Agnes, kneeling before him and meeting unflinchingly his reproving look. "Oh, father, I cannot tell you how beautiful a soul is straying from heaven in that Lel whom you fear. I know she wishes to change my present purpose, I know she came here chiefly to alter my determination, I know she expects my visit to her to promote or accomplish her object. But I have found out that she is less attached to the world than I am to the cloister, that she would sooner relinquish her idols than I the veil. In the struggle between us the victory will be mine, not hers. For this I wish to go."

The priest regarded her a while in silence, and then said, with a smile of compassion and love, —

"Is this your only reason, my child?"

"It is, indeed. If there be in my heart one lurking wish to see or share the pleasures I have heard of, but never tasted; if there be one spark of curiosity to know something of life's pageantry before I leave it; if there be any motive other than that I have mentioned. before heaven I am unconscious of it. "

"My child, my child, your motive is beautiful. But your generous designs will plunge you into temptations which it would be presumption to seek without a special call."

"Father," said the young girl, her dark eye gleaming with radiance beyond that which men call beauty, "Father, it is not merely because I have been educated in a convent school, screened from conventional blandishments by the solitudes of Loretto, and accustomed from infancy to the impressive observances of this consecrated retreat, that I have determined to be a religious. I have heard my schoolmates picture their city homes and pastimes in colors brighter, perhaps, than reality. The finger of God has pointed out my vocation, and my choice is unalterably made. As I recognized his blessed hand when I first announced to you my fixed resolve, so do I now recognize his sacred voice, and it bids me go. "

Agnes still knelt, her hands clasped, her face upturned to heaven, as if bearing witness to her truth. It was a beautful group — the priest and the mother in tears, the daughter's lips parted with something holier than a smile.

"Yes," she fervently continued, kissing her confessor's hand, "let me begin my mission now."

"Come to me after the Angelus, bring your cousin and her friend; if I permit you then, remember, it will the exception, not the rule."

One by one the candles on the altar were lighted, and Melville could see Lel, kneeling or leaning forward, he knew not which; but still there was no sign of Agnes. Presently a sweet-toned bell began to ring, and then a rustling was heard, as a hundred girls, two by two, and a hundred sisters, entered the chapel. Melville had bestowed only a careless glance on the exquisite marble work of the altar, and was examining a fine painting in the gleam on the opposite wall, when a figure appeared through the side door of the sacristy and knelt in the front seat. It was Agnes! But never till then had Melville seen the expression at which he wondered kindled into such active power; it was as if a bud, already marked as the fairest in the garden, had burst into a flower more rare,

more fragrant, more beautiful than all the promise of spring. The mellow light streamed full
on her face, revealing the glory which invests
the body, when, detached from earth without
the bitterness of death, the soul mounts on the
wings of faith to commune with its Redeemer.
He could not turn away from the apparition, he
feared lest it should disappear, it was so spiritual, so unreal, so angelical. Agnes knew not
that any human eye was on her, for her own
was on heaven; but Lel knew it.

The folding doors of the sacristy opened, the
confessor, unattended, knelt before the blessed
sacrament, the Litany of MARY began. With
the deep swell of the organ came a clear, soft
voice, intoning, those dear, dear, ever dear epi-
thets which the sanctity of ages has lovingly
and humbly bestowed on the Virgin Mother of
JESUS, whilst the choir responded in unison,
" *Ora pro nobis!* "

And when the chanting ceased the convent
bell again was heard, and the *Angelus* went
murmuring from the altar to the choir. The
ceremony was over; too soon for Lel, too soon
for Melville, upon whom it left an impression of.
profound sadness.

Agnes had displayed so much penetration and
resolution that her confessor was more than half

inclined to yield the point, but well knowing the seraphic shapes in which the subtle fiend deludes innocence he deemed it more prudent to withhold a decision until he had seen Lel.

He had not long to wait before she entered with Agnes, followed by Melville and Mrs. Cleveland. After the ordinary greetings of first acquaintance, he conducted them from the sacristy to a room in a small brick house adjoining the church, and bade them warm themselves whilst he placed wine and cake on the table. As Mrs. Cleveland approached to assist him he whispered, —

"Is that young gentleman a relative?"

"Engaged to my niece, I believe."

"Ag," said Lel, looking from the ceiling to to the floor, and scrutinizing the window sashes, "were we not here once before?"

"More than once," replied Agnes.

"But you were not here then?" resumed Lel, appealing to the confessor.

"No, Miss Almy, or I should remember you."

"And I should remember you, though I must have been a very little girl then. What has become of your predecessor, the old gentleman in spectacles, who looked like a prophet, and told me that I would one day be a better Catholic than Agnes?"

"Father Thomas," suggested Agnes.

"Yes!" cried Lel, eagerly, as the name recalled his image more vividly.

"He is enjoying, I trust, the full reward of his pious labors," answered the priest, "and perhaps praying now amidst the angels for the fulfilment of his prophecy. Miss Almy," he continued, presenting her a glass of wine, "there is a milk-white lamb amongst these hills, whom we love and watch most tenderly, and you have come to steal her from us."

Lel was silent.

"You have made her believe that our country fields afford poor nourishment, and taught her to sigh for more alluring pastures."

Lel was silent, Melville restless.

"You would have her forsake the simple herbage that has hitherto sustained her, to crop the hot-house plants which may poison as soon as tasted."

"You do her too much injustice," objected Melville.

"Are you too in the conspiracy, Mr. Melville? There are four against me then," retorted the confessor, looking from one to the other."

"As suppliants only, not extortioners," added Lel, turning away as if to examine a proof engraving of the Last Supper.

The good priest had at last made up his mind, and taking Agnes by the hand, he said,—

"And for how long, my child, would you leave us?"

"For a month."

"Miss Almy, you must turn your back on me no longer. I own myself vanquished and commit your cousin to your keeping for a month!"

Melville bowed deeply, and thanked him cordially, whilst Agnes crossed over to Lel, who was still examining the picture.

"Why, Lel!" exclaimed Agnes, completely taken by surprise, as Lel, who had been vainly struggling with her tears, fell weeping on her neck.

"Strange, strange girl," murmured Melville to himself. "When shall I ever know her real character!"

"Tears of joy, my child?" inquired the confessor, touched by her emotion.

"No, sir," cried Lel, "tears of sorrow! I could not ask your consent because in my inmost soul I did not wish it. Up to this moment I have labored incessantly to induce Agnes to accompany me home, but my heart failed me at the dawn of success; and were I not prevented by" — her promise to her uncle flashed across her, — "by — by violating every rule of propriety and respect, I would supplicate you now to retract your permission."

"Which I should never do," said the priest, who saw the beautiful soul of which Agnes spoke, shining through the tears in Lel's eyes.

"Place her not in my keeping!" continued Lel, with mournful earnestness, "I am not worthy of so holy a charge!"

"Then in God's keeping! I relieve you of responsibility;" and from that moment the name of Ellen Almy became an altar-word; and throughout that peaceful convent there were prayers offered up from many a pure heart for her peace and happiness.

CHAPTER VII.

THAT night Lel had a dream. She dreamed that she was in the Convent Chapel, alone — at midnight; that as she was kneeling there, a lady, whose face was concealed by a white veil spangled with stars, appeared upon the altar. Slowly and noiselessly the figure moved towards her and stood over her, the veil was uplifted — it was her mother! Not the pale, cold body she had seen in the coffin, but the mild, warm, bright being, whose breast had once been her home, the living mother of other days. She dreamed that her mother kissed her, saying, " I have come to life again, you are no longer motherless; though invisible, I will be ever at your side to hear your lowest whisper, and grant whatever a parent's love may bestow. Sleeping or waking, I shall watch over you, go where you will I am with you, and though years and years may pass before we meet again, remember that your mother lives!"

The figure receded to the altar, as if wafted back by unseen wings; a smile of more than mortal sweetness overspread her face, and from her hands and forehead streamed forth rays of glory, bathing the sanctuary in light. It was still her mother's form, but not her mother, not the mother who had died; but one like her, only far more beautiful, far more powerful, and in loving whom she had loved her parent, too. It was still her mother, but more than her mother!

" O Holy One, leave me not!" trembled on her lips, as the lovely vision seemed about to lose itself in excess of light; but in the effort to speak she awoke with a Christmas sun beaming full on her face. It was nine o'clock.

" I thought you were never going to wake,"

said Agnes. " Do you know that you have been crying in your sleep ? "

" Oh ! I have had such a dream," sighed Lel, pressing the tears from her eyelids. " I dreamed that my mother was living and appeared to me; how beautiful she was ! And now that you smile, you remind me of the look she gave me as she vanished. Ag, when I first woke and saw you kneeling there I thought you were an angel."

" I wish I were, Lel, if only to be your guardian."

" What have you been doing to yourself this morning ? "

" Nothing. What do you mean ? "

" Have you been riding ? " pursued Lel, after a pause.

" I rode to the Convent with mother."

" What took you there so early ? "

" To go to communion."

" To communion," murmured Lel, resting her cheek on her hand; then turning fondly to her friend, she said, " Agnes, do you think that if I had been to communion I should look as you do now ? If I thought so I might — Do you really mean to go home with me to-morrow ? "

" Yes," replied Agnes, laughing.

" Yes ? " echoed Lel, adding sadly and slowly, " May I never hear music again if I am not sorry for it ! "

The Colonel was getting ready for church. Christmas, he said, was one of the few festivals in the year when it became imperative on every thorough-bred gentleman to appear in his pew, just to show that Christianity was a very good thing in its way, and to encourage the lower classes in their harmless devotions. There was a smack of vulgarity in staying home on such an occasion ; it savored of false aristocracy ; men ought to concede something to the practice of their ancestors and the prejudices of their neighbors ; in short, he owed it to himself and the community to go to church. A landholder of liberal tastes and fine impulses was, of course, not required to hear mass as regularly as a daily laborer or a woman ; but still it was incumbent on every admirer of the Gospel to make some public acknowledgment, once in a while, of his respect for Christianity and his want of sympathy with atheism. Besides this, there was a drop of Catholic blood in the old man's heart, which ran thrilling through his veins at the sound of the Christmas mass-bell, startling his well-contented conscience an instant from its slumbers.

The Colonel had already bestowed an hour on his toilet, and with Charley's assistance it was nearly complete.   Touched by the keen edge of his favorite razor, his chin was as smooth as an infant's, his hair was richly powdered, his white cravat tied in faultless symmetry.   No wonder he stood before the glass so complacently arranging his ruffles, whilst Charley brushed his best coat, for he was hale, hearty, and handsome; and, with his well-turned limbs, his imposing carriage, his rich complexion, so peculiar to the gentleman epicure, his fine head and delicate hands, he was at that moment a study for an artist.

"Brush it well, my boy," said the Colonel, anxious to be seen to all possible advantage; for he knew that his appearance in church was expected by all the parish; that his entrance could not in the nature of things be unobserved; that after service every eye would be on him.

"Not a speck!" cried the old man, diligently examining the coat and taking a gold-piece from his waistcoat pocket.   "Have you heard mass, Charley?"

"Yes, sir; three masses."

"That's right."

"And I went to communion with mistress."

"You're a good boy, Charley," giving him the

gold-piece. " Why, you bow equal to a dancing-master or a Muscovy duck. Now get my hat — I wish it were a few years younger — but it will do — it will do.

"I never saw you look so well in my life, sir," whispered Charley, timidly, as he dexterously applied the brush for the last time, and drew back to contemplate his master in humble admiration.

"Ha! ha!" laughed the Colonel, not at all displeased; " I thank you for the Christmas gift, especially," he internally concluded, " as it is not undeserved. Now, my boy, get the carriage. I will drive. I expect to find dinner and the presents *comme il faut* on my return!"

" *Comme il faut!* " replied Charley, who had the words like a parrot.

"Stop! my cane!" — another glance in the mirror, another rub of the chin, another pull at his waistbands, and the Colonel was *ready for church.*

A Christmas Mass is always beautiful; beautiful in the Cathedral, where nave and aisle are crowded with the rich and poor, thronging to hear " *the glad tidings;* " where a thousand faces are beaming in reverent joy, as amid incense and immortal music the pontifical ceremonies proceed; beautiful in the country church, where a

single priest intones the same unchanging service,
where many a youth and maiden, many a father
and mother in the decline of life, who have walked
six miles or more, fasting, are humbly expecting
Communion, with a holy earnestness, through
which no trace of corporal fatigue is seen ; but
still more beautiful is it in a Convent Chapel,
with the whole community assembled to hail the
Nativity of the infant JESUS, one of the glorious
feasts for which they have renounced earth's
meaner banquets, one of the blessed days which
more than repay them for the brittle trinkets
they have resigned.   Take the rapture of the
queen of beauty when the ball is at its height,—
take the exultation of a true-hearted patriot, or
the feigned transports of a maudlin politician on
some time-honored national holiday — combine
both, yet how poor, how false, how feeble are
they if contrasted with the calm delight felt by a
religious community when celebrating the grand
festivals of the Church ! Christmas is not the
time to pity the recluse ; and even the Colonel.
after an attentive perusal of the blissful faces
before him, wondered how so much sweet content, so much radiant joy, could lurk beneath a
sister's plain black cap, and had a better opinion
of the cloister.

The service was over ; the small congregation

gathered round their pastor, who had a smile, a word, a blessing for all; for the aged men and women who shook his hands; for the young who blushed as he saluted them; for the urchins who clung laughing to his cassock, begging for their pictures and their medals.

Nor was the Colonel forgotten. Deeply as he bowed to the confessor, he was careful to preserve the demeanor of one who was conferring quite as great an honor as he received. And oh! his air of inimitable, and well-nigh imperceptible condescension, when patting his country friends familiarly on the shoulder, he said in measured syllables, as they approached him in regular file: "I expect you all at Loretto."

During this scene, the confessor had beckoned Agnes into the sacristy to say a few parting words. When they came forth, Agnes was weeping, and Lel's keen eye could detect the ghost of a tear, as she called it, wandering over the good old father's cheek.

"Good-by!" It was soon said, but long remembered.

"What's that on the porch?" inquired Lel, as they neared Loretto; "and why are all these people following us?"

The Colonel smiled sagaciously. Lel, still staring in amazement, continued, "Uncle, upon my

word, your cottage has been metamorphosed into
an admiral's flag-ship."

She sprang from the carriage as soon as it
stopped, and found a tall Christmas bush at each
end of the porch; whilst shawls, cloaks, comforts,
blankets, swung in festoons from the ropes con-
necting the columns.

"What in the name of all that's most mysterious is the meaning of this?" ejaculated the bewildered girl. "Do you mean to have a fancy
ball?"

But the mystery was soon unravelled, as the
whole population of the district, young and old,
seemed to pour itself into Loretto. It was the
Colonel's Christmas-gift to the neighborhood.

The Colonel stood on the nicely gravelled
walk, his hand thrust blandly into his buff waistcoat, whilst Charley and Mrs. Cleveland unrobed
the bushes for the children, and presented the
more serviceable gifts — each was labelled — to
its owner. And here Charley and the Colonel re-
versed their position in the trout season; for
during the distribution, the Colonel spoke of
the crops, the weather, the country assizes, the
European news, the scarcity of partridges, without seeming to have the slightest interest in
what was going on, whilst Charley claimed all
the thanks and smiles as pompously and perti-

naciously as if he had been the real benefactor.
But in truth it was a spectacle worth contem-
plating; reminding one of the times when such
acts of benevolence were daily witnessed at the
abbey gates, which are now in ruins, or closed to
all who come in poverty instead of titled splendor.

Whether through Charley or the Colonel, or
from Lel herself, it was soon ascertained that
Agnes would leave in the morning for the city;
and all their joy was turned to sorrow. Tears
clouded the eyes which had been brightly beaming, and she could scarcely pacify them by promising a speedy return; for they loved her to
jealousy and feared to lose her. Lel, perceiving
from the dark looks cast on her, that she had
become an object of suspicion and dislike, retreated into the parlor, saying to Melville, —

"I shall be mobbed if I remain."

Nor did she venture forth until the crowd had
dispersed, and Charley was taking down the
bare ropes.

"Well!" cried Lel, playing with her uncle's
ruffle, "if you are not original there's no eccen-
tricity on the face of the earth. Am I in fairy-
land? When shall I forget this memorable visit
to Loretto?"

"*Never!*" whispered a low voice in her ear,
and she felt her cousin's lips on her cheek.

CHAPTER VIII.

RS. CLEVELAND, Melville, and Agnes, were at vespers; Lel and her uncle had the cottage to themselves.

"What ails you, pet?" said the Colonel; "you are pale."

"I have a headache," replied Lel.

"Is that all? I have a homœopathic pill up-stairs that will cure you, in five minutes."

"Stop, uncle," said Lel, detaining him, "have you one that will cure the heartache, too?"

"Eh!" whispered the old gentleman, with a most knowing look, drawing closer to his niece, "are *you* afflicted with the heartache? *You*, my rattling, prattling, romping, laughing, merry, mischief-making mistress? Come. I'll cure you in half an hour; put on your bonnet."

"A walk!" cried Lel, who longed for the fresh air.

Arm-in-arm they sallied forth. The afternoon was as mild and bright as the spring, and the horizon was wrapped in a deep, mellow haze. They soon left the road for a path that wound up the hill, and here, for better walking, they had to part company. For a time the Colonel led the way with more agility and ease than

one would imagine, plying his stick with the
dexterity of a Swiss mountaineer. Lel followed
quietly until near the summit, then at every
step her eye and cheek grew brighter and
brighter, and passing her uncle with a bound,
she sprang forward like a deer towards the high
rock that crowned the hill. While he was still
panting and puffing up the ascent Lel had
climbed the rock. There she stood, balanced
on a sharp splinter of stone, all glowing from
the exercise, her bonnet dangling from her
wrist, her hair breaking from its golden coil to
sweep over her neck.

"Now I can breathe," she exclaimed, extending her arms as if to embrace the free air, and
glancing down on the wide circle beneath her,
"now I can breathe."

The Colonel was by no means poetical, yet it
cost him some minutes to persuade himself that
the aerial figure before him so clearly marked
against the flushing western sky was his own
niece Lel; and he could not help believing that
had he been twenty years younger he would
have fled in terror and reported the hill as
sacred as Parnassus.

"How's the heartache, Lel?" he cried, climbing to her side.

"Better."

"And the headache?"

"Gone. But I am ruined, ruined, utterly ruined. I shall never love the city again; Loretto has.poisoned my home; my heart is among these hills. See how the sun plunges into that gorge, making those bare trees beautiful; see how it runs a race with your trout stream, capering there through those velvet fields of young wheat."

"So ho!" shouted the Colonel, as she paused. "My young enthusiast, methinks I see you in your father's parlor shaking off our dust .from your feet, and solemnly vowing never again to visit our barbarous solitude. Isn't it so?" asked the Colonel, expecting an impassioned negative, — and he got it.

"But," continued Lel, dropping her head, "in a few weeks I should forget you all and have as keen a relish for morning calls and evening balls as I had before. I should have nothing on my conscience; and now and then a sweet recollection of the cottage, the convent, or this hill might steal over me and be a cordial for the the heartache. But now "——

"What's on your conscience now?" said the Colonel, playfully.

"Agnes," replied Lel. "Uncle, *must* I keep the promise I have made you?"

"No, certainly not," muttered the Colonel, coldly. "I have no authority to *compel* you to oblige me."

"But you have power," returned Lel, looking him steadily in the face, "you have power to compel me to sacrifice myself to save you."

"Then, far be it from me to exercise a power in which I can take so little pride or pleasure."

"Let her stay, then, uncle, I beseech you. Tell her that, at the last moment, you cannot consent to part with her. Dear, dear uncle, do this and save her, save me. You may have her back a woman of the world, but never, never as she is now."

"Nonsense," cried the Colonel. "Isn't it a woman's business on earth to be a woman of the world? Do you want her to be a woman of the sun, the moon, the stars? Do you want her to stand apart from humanity, a cold, unfamiliar, uninstructed, uncongenial thing, a being out of place, an isolated unit? Give me a woman who possesses all the graces with which the refinement of centuries has adorned polite society; whose words, motions, actions are tuned to ease and elegance; who polishes her manners for the delight of all, and instructs her heart for the love of one. Such is a woman of the world, and honored be the title."

"Such may be a woman of the world," said Lel; "but I would rather be a milkmaid, untutored and neglected, with one true friend to love me, than shine as a woman of the world from now till doomsday. Uncle, I have some experience, and I am inclined to think a woman of the world one of the-humbugs of the day."

"What are *you*, then?" rejoined the Colonel, tartly.

"As complete a humbug as ever existed; and yet I'm only an approximation to a woman of the world. Some years hence, if I remain single, my education shall be perfected; I shall then have condensed into this little body of mine the congregated graces of nineteen centuries; I shall subdue impulse and be elegant by rule, fascinate my friends by my manners, and win a husband by my interior worth."

"You misrepresent and mock me, girl," said the Colonel, sternly and sadly.

"Then forgive me," said Lel, kissing him. "What I mean to say is this: that in the fashionable life to which I must introduce Agnes there is such a decided preponderance of the bad and silly over the good and elegant that she will lose more than she gains. I admit that I love the life I have been leading, that I would not willingly resign it; it is only at times that

I feel, as now I do, the emptiness, the nothingness of our pomp and etiquette, but when the
feeling comes, I despise myself."

"Most unreasonably."

"Perhaps so.   But Agnes is not made for this
world."

"Is she made for a convent?"

"It seems to me that she is made to spend
her days at Loretto, and die as she closes your
old eyes."

"Lel," began the Colonel, with much hesita-
tion, "be candid. Have you not some other
reason for wishing your cousin to remain here?"

"None!" said Lel, as unsuspecting as a child.

"None?" repeated the Colonel, with a searching gaze.

"Look deep," said Lel, laughing, though her
neck arched slightly, "look deep and read what
you can see!"

"I read," resumed the Colonel, in a whisper,
"that Agnes Cleveland is beautiful — that George
Melville sees it — that Ellen Almy fears it."

Lel's face was crimson in an instant, and then
pale as death, as she muttered indignantly, —

"*Fear it!*" and stood motionless, as if rooted
to the rock. Then, with a flashing eye and quivering lip, she slowly raised her finger, and scan-
ning the Colonel from head to foot, until he

fairly quailed, exclaimed, half in pity and half in anger,—

"Oh uncle, uncle!"

"I was jesting, Lel," he said, approaching her.

"*You were not!*" she cried, as the warm blood rushed back to her cheeks. "But let it pass." And without another syllable she tied her bonnet on and descended the rock, the Colonel following sadly and silently. Not a word passed between them until they gained the road, though they walked side by side. The Colonel was breathing heavily, as if unusually fatigued, and he coughed almost incessantly. Lel, remarking it, slackened her pace to watch him as he passed her. She could not see his face well, for his head was deeply inclined; but she could see his hand, ever and anon, nervously applied to his eyes. Her very soul melted at the sight, and stealing close to his side she laid her hand upon his shoulder. He started as if stung by a serpent, and catching the merciful gleam of Lel's clear, loving eye, pressed her with a long sob to his bosom.

"Oh, my child, my child, forgive me!" was all he could say. But this was enough, more than enough for the generous girl.

"I was a fool to mind you," she said, "and worse than a fool to fly at you like a blind bat."

"I thought you a woman," he added, "but you are more than a woman!"

"Not more than a woman, uncle; only more than a woman of the world."

Thus saying, she wound her arm around his, and sang for him until they reached the white palings of Loretto.

Mrs. Cleveland, Agnes, and Melville had returned from vespers and were grouped around the fire. But it was no longer the same cheerful group we have more than once described; a shadow had fallen on the hearth; the note of the crackling wood was more like a sigh than a song. Lel made no attempt at merriment; she found the silence so much more grateful than conversation. Now and then a trivial question and answer was exchanged; but it meant nothing. Though each saw that the other was thinking of the morrow, they knew that it required but a word to conjure up the parting scene too vividly; so, in mutual charity, they carefully avoided the subject. Agnes, herself, seemed to feel the least. It may have been that she did not realize the coming separation; that to her, as to most young persons, there was a vague sense of pleasure in any change, or that resignation and hope rendered her calmer. Thus passed a very long hour.

'We cannot dwell on an evening like this; it is better imagined 'than described. After tea Melville and the Colonel played chess, whilst Mrs. Cleveland sat between her daughter and her niece. She addressed herself chiefly to Lel, and, with all a mother's tenderness and minuteness, described the course she wished her to observe towards Agnes; for though the separation was to be brief, it was the first experiment, and suggested a multitude of fears. And besides this, Agnes was peculiarly circumstanced, and might feel no inclination to participate in the amusements which others found so delightful. She did not think it necessary to apprise Lel of her daughter's intention; most likely, as Agnes believed, the Colonel had already told her.

Lel trembled as the anxious mother spoke of the confidence she reposed in her judgment, sincerity, and love; of the sacredness of the treasure she was about to entrust her with. Her sole reply was to press her aunt's hand to her lips as Agnes and her mother rose to leave the room. We shall not follow them. It is well at times, like the ancient artist, to veil the workings of a parent's heart.

Lel had a never-failing friend and comforter in the piano. At home it served to chase away many a sad thought, and she found it equally valuable at Loretto. She opened it, instinctively, and began to play. Melville, by dint of constant watchfulness and reflection, had contrived to let the Colonel beat him. But, as may have been noticed, Lel's music laid a spell on him. His attention was entirely withdrawn from the game, and, playing without proper precaution, he made such havoc with the old man's pieces as nearly to cost him the Colonel's good opinion.

However, the night was wearing away; the piano was closed; the mimic armies slept peacefully in the same tent. Lel had scarcely entered her room when she heard a tap at the door. It was the Colonel; he held in his hand a string of pearls which he threw around her neck. Many a lady would have received it, many rejected it as a bribe; but Lel, with truer feeling, recognized it as a peace offering, which it were false pride or cruelty to reject.

"You have made me a promise, Lel," he said, patting her on the head, "a promise which you repent. I release you from it, and trust all to your own good heart."

Before she could reply he had left the room. A load was taken from her heart; the thorn was plucked from her pillow; and long before Agnes left her mother she was sleeping happily.

They breakfasted by candle-light, for the roads

wcre bad, and they had to take the stage at seven. Charley's eyes swam as he handed the coffee around.

"Charley," said the Colonel, "I believe you like Miss Agnes more than me."

"No, I don't, sir," stammered the boy; "I'd cry more for her, but I'd do more for you."

"Then be sure you are in time for the stage."

The carriage was at the door. "Not a minute to spare," cried the Colonel, tearing Agnes from her mother's arms. "You are not parting for a century. Let her go, sister, she's not going round Cape Horn. Good-by, Melville, God bless you, sir; you know where to find us again. The trout will soon be at us — fine place this in spring and summer; much pleasanter than now — no comparison, I assure you. Do come, do come. Good-by, Lel; good-by, Agnes; be good girls. Take care of 'em, Melville. There you are. Now, Charley, off we go. Good-by!"

The whip cracked, the carriage rolled away. The Colonel stood on the porch until they were out of sight, and then, embracing his sister tenderly, led her into the desolate parlor, and, seating himself by her side, whispered in her ear, —

"Come, Mary, cheer up! We are not too old to be just as happy together, now, as we have been for many a year."

CHAPTER IX.

IN the breakfast-room of a large house in the most fashionable part of a large city sat Lel's father.   He had just taken tea alone, and was reading the evening paper by the light of a well-modeled Carcel lamp.   He was a middle-aged man, small, but firmly knit; his keen gray eye, naturally quick, was so characterized by habit that a stranger might honor him at sight for a shrewd, successful man of business.   There was nothing repulsive either in his face or person; yet nothing positively attractive. He lacked the Colonel's friendly air, his beaming smile of universal benevolence; in fact, there were no indications of philanthropy in Mr. Almy's appearance.   Yet, on 'change, no one was more honored for his fairness and high-toned liberality; no one more respected for his accurate and extensive information; no one more envied for his uniform success.   Whenever blamed, it was for too much indulgence to his friends, or too much boldness in his operations.   Yet a very close observer might have taken him for a mixture of the miser and the cynic, artfully disguised beneath a well-contrived surface of self-sustaining dignity.

He had acquired great command over his countenance, which, usually, was composed, not placid —there is a vast difference. But now there seemed to be something painful on his mind; for, at times, he dropped the paper and would lose himself in thoughts, from which he started with a sigh. During one of these reveries a carriage stopped at the front door; he did not hear it.

"Here we are, Agnes!" cried Lel.

Agnes found herself before a stately dwelling, whose pillared entrance looked out upon a noble city, stretching proudly away to the distant river glittering in the moonlight. The door flew open, and Lel, darting into the breakfast-room, threw her arms around her father's neck. He kissed her gently—to Agnes it seemed coldly— on the forehead, and then welcomed Melville so cordially that our novice was surprised at the contrast. He had seen Agnes—few things escaped his quick vision—and, judging from her plain dress and timid bearing, thought her a waiting-maid whom his eccentric child had imported from Loretto until Lel thus undeceived him.

"My dear father, there is the sweetest creature that mortal eye ever rested on, in your niece, Agnes Cleveland."

Mr. Almy took a good long look at her, then kissed her, saying, —

"You are most welcome, and we shall all try to make you happy."

Accustomed to warmer language Agnes felt her heart sink within her, yet she managed to smile a reply. At this moment another was added to the group. No one saw him enter; yet there he stood amongst them. He was small, delicately made, very pale and spare, and for one so young seemed to have suffered much hard treatment. He reminded Agnes of some one who was familiar to her; but the person she remembered, whoever it was, had a bright, laughing face, and this stranger was sad almost to severity. Still there was a striking resemblance, which increased as he smiled on her. What his relations were to the Almys never clearly appeared; he was one of the household, with this peculiarity, that he disappeared with Lel and was sure to return with her; but where he went remained a mystery.

"I knew you would be here to meet me," said Lel, taking his hand.

"I was nearly prevented," he replied; and Agnes noticed that he spoke in a whisper.

"My cousin, Gabriel," resumed Lel, introducing him to Agnes; "he rarely speaks above a whisper. You are now acquainted with the whole family."

There was something interesting in Gabriel which at once attached Agnes to him; and whenever he looked on her she thought his expression softened, thus increasing the likeness she had remarked. Mr. Almy was a little impatient of his presence, and seemed to consider it an intrusion; whilst Melville remained perfectly indifferent.

Gabriel took no part in the conversation; and in the midst of it would doze soundly for some minutes, then wake up and doze again. Once, as his head drooped, Agnes touched Lel.

"Poor fellow!" sighed Lel, "they say he has a disease of the heart. This drowsiness is one of the symptoms. But come; you must be tired, for I can hardly keep my eyes open. Excuse us, gentlemen. Good night!"

Gabriel left the room with them.

"Now for a chat, Melville," said Mr. Almy, producing a decanter of gin; "but first, what sort of a girl is my niece?"

"A very superior woman, I assure you."

"Glad to hear it," said the merchant; "I thought as much. Plain looking, eh?"

"Do you think so?" returned Melville, in unfeigned astonishment.

"Well — yes — rather," pursued Mr. Almy, sipping his toddy. "If she can take a polish,

though, she is in good hands now. Have you
seen the news from Europe — confoundedly
black!" — and no further allusion was made to
Agnes.

Mr. Almy had a sincere regard for Melville;
he prized him for his generous nature, and
respected him as a man of the purest honor. He
was never happier than when talking with
Melville, whose strong, lucid mind cast a light
on every subject he touched, whether political,
social, moral, or commercial. After the labors
of the day it was delightful for Mr. Almy thus to
recreate himself, and gradually reduce his excit-
able nerves to a pleasant repose by the united
efficacy of new ideas and old Schiedam. However, Mr. Almy found very little entertainment
or instruction in Melville that evening; he was
often guilty of the most provoking inattention,
the most absurd opinions; and he confessed that
the train of his ideas, as often befel him in
travelling, was off the track.

As such dialogues are not very entertaining
we shift the scene, with this single remark: that
Mr. Almy did not mention himself unavoidably
once, and that Melville, though familiar with
his opinions, was not admitted within the well-
guarded circle of his feelings. Or more briefly
and more intelligibly, they were rather com-

panions than friends, in business and politics communicative enough, but silent about themselves.

"The Colonel has *his* sanctum, and this is mine," said Lel, as she ushered Agnes into a room communicating with her chamber. The room looked like Lel, and contained conveniences and embellishments enough to make most girls of fashion uninterruptedly happy. Yet it was here, on that tempting lounge, that Lel spent many a dismal hour. She was never so sad as when she mused there all by herself, after breakfast or after an evening feast. Still, she loved her quiet sanctuary; for its very sadness was refreshing and salutary.

Poor Agnes! the exquisite beauty and finish of the apartment only served to picture more vividly, in contrast, the plain parlor at Loretto. She struggled hard against it, but nature was too strong in her young heart, and she burst into tears. To Lel, crying was as natural as laughing; but Agnes rarely wept, and had parted from her mother with only a sigh. This natural, but sudden heart-break was thus so painful to Lel that even the duty of consoling — that mainspring of the female heart — could not prevent her from mingling her tears with her cousin's.

"No wonder you cry, Ag," she said; "there's no rejoicing fire here to welcome us with a merry volley, or to bark at our feet like a faithful dog; but, instead of this, the hot air comes sneaking up through those miserable apertures, breathing a sickly heat, as if the winter had a fever. If I live to see to-morrow I'll have a fireplace cut somewhere, though we have to run the chimney horizontally out of that window."

Lel soon succeeded in making Agnes laugh, and when she thought the danger of a relapse over, asked her with an air of inimitable drollery, —

"What do you think of my father?"

This was too categorical for an answer.

"Very unlike the Colonel, isn't he?"

Agnes assented.

"Don't you find his manner cold and unprepossessing?"

"How can I answer you, Lel?"

"By telling the truth."

"But how can I know the truth in a glance?"

"Poh! no evasion; Melville would call you a special pleader. Were you not disappointed in him?"

"If you *must* have it," said Agnes, laughing, "I scarcely noticed him after Gabriel came into the room."

"Never mind Gabriel now. Answer me, were you not disappointed?"

"Yes."

"I knew you would be. If I had met such a man at Loretto without knowing him he would have congealed me into an icicle in five minutes."

"How can you speak of your father so?" said Agnes, whose fine organ of reverence was shocked.

"How can I speak of him otherwise?" returned Lel; "he's so much better than he looks that I'm ashamed of his appearance. Agnes, I'll bet you all the hair on my head against a lock of yours that you love him in less than a fortnight. I could make you love him now if I were to enumerate all his acts of devotion to me; I've forgotten more than half, but what I remember would compel your affection."

"I'm sure of it," said Agnes, earnestly.

"Why," resumed Lel, warming as she spoke, "he was left a widower at thirty; all his habits and feelings inclined him to matrimony, and he could have chosen from the proudest and fairest in the land, for he was young, rich, and gifted. But he did not marry, he repelled all advances; why? because a wayward little girl was left him, love's only legacy; because the spoiled child would have withered under a new mother, because he prized the young creature's happiness above his own, because he loved his daughter better than himself. *I* am that legacy, and I have seen the battle and the victory."

"You have reason to love him," said Agnes.

"Indeed I have!" exclaimed Lel, with fervor. "But could I tell you how he abstained from all a bachelor's amusements to spend the long evenings with that motherless child; how he appropriated her first affections to himself instead of permitting them to fasten on a nurse, as most men do and ever will do; how he declined and still declines all invitations to clubs, dinners, matches, and to all the amusements he loves, that he may stay at home and be what a father ought to be; oh, Agnes, the mere recital would enchant you!"

"Lel, dear Lel, I believe you."

"I am not overdrawing the picture, Agnes, nor am I blinded by filial love. I might talk till doomsday without doing him justice, and when I begin to speak of him I know not when to stop. But you must pardon me; I would not utter a syllable in his praise if his hypocritical face did not compel me to give it the lie; it is eternally saying, 'here is a cold-blooded, calculating spec-

ulator,' when it ought to say, 'here is a self-denying, generous, loving father.' I cannot account
for the variance between his disposition and appearance; I have been trying for five years, but
why his interior virtue has not some outward sign
is still a riddle. Why, mercy on me! my own
little face is a passport to everybody's confidence;
I hear more secrets than any body in town, yet
my heart is no more to be compared to my
father's than it is to your mother's."

"I won't take your bet, Lel," said Agnes, embracing her friend; "you have made me love
him already."

"I don't want you to love him on my words,
but on your own careful observation. I have
great reliance on your sagacity, and you must
assist me to explain the contradiction between
his heart and his face. I have drawn all sorts of
pictures of him, and with the same set of features
I can give the expression he *ought* to have; the
expression I have sometimes caught, flashing an
instant, then vanishing like a meteor."

"Do you think he will like me?" Agnes asked,
"for I cannot study him to advantage unless he
does."

"He likes you already," cried Lel, "or he
never would have said what he did."

"He could not have said less."

"But he might have said a great deal more, and meant a great deal less."

Here the conversation ceased, and Lel thought that Agnes must have fallen asleep on her knees, her prayers were so unreasonably long.

CHAPTER X.

ERE you ever at a concert, Ag?"

"Never."

"Wouldn't you like to hear Beethoven's Symphony in C Minor?"

"Yes!" cried Agnes, joyously, who, until introduced by Lel to the great master, had reverenced him only as a mighty shade, standing afar off in the mist and majesty of distance like one of Ossian's heroes.

"Come, then, we've no time to lose;" and away they went to the boudoir. "What are you going to wear, Ag?"

"Am I expected to wear anything more?"

"Why, you're not going in that dress; it doesn't fit."

"It fits quite well enough; mother made it."

"Yes, mothers can do a great many things for their daughters, but they can't make their dresses."

"Then I'll stay at home. I thought Beethoven might be heard without a ticket from a mantua-maker."

"No ; that's a necessary preliminary," replied Lel, without relaxing a muscle. "But I can fix you in three minutes. Look here," she continued, producing a cream-colored sack, or opera cloak, and rapidly passing it on her cousin's arms. "Now, a white japonica in your hair, and you'll do."

" No, no," said Agnes, escaping from the sack. " I couldn't listen with this mealy shroud around me."

"It *is* hard to civilize you savages," retorted Lel, partially vexed at the cool contempt with which Agnes disposed of her cloak.

Whilst talking, she had made her own toilet as plain as possible, to avoid a contrast.

" Just one flower in your hair," continued Lel.

" No."

"Aggie, my dear, dear Aggie, for *my* sake, just this teeny tiny bud," said Lel, kneeling in irresistible humility.

"Well," and the flower rested lovingly on her dark hair.

"Murder ! murder !" screamed Lel, as Agnes began to put her bonnet on, " you irreclaimable barbarian ! "

"Are we going bareheaded ? "

"Of course we are. How else can we hear?" said Lel, casting down her eyes.

"How else can we be seen ? you would say. I *will* wear it."

"Then *I'll* stay at home. Agnes, listen to me; however much you may despise fashion, yet your good sense will teach you that conformity to an innocent custom is better than unnecessary defiance. A bonnet in a concert-room is as ridiculous as satin and tarletan in the country."

"So be it, then," murmured Agnes, dropping her bonnet in despair.

"That's a darling," cried Lel, kissing her and throwing a white nubia over cousin's shoulders. "There'll be a crowd; come, or father and Melville will suspect that mirror of detaining us."

"Shall we walk or ride?" said Mr. Almy.

"Oh, walk, walk, by all means walk. What's the use of wasting moonlight in a carriage," replied Lel, about to take her father's arm.

"No, my dear," said Mr. Almy, offering his arm to Agnes, and giving her a large bouquet, "I prefer your cousin."

Lel's entrance created almost universal commotion. "*There's Lel! There's Lel!*" passed from mouth to mouth until every eye was on her. Everybody seemed glad to see her — old ladies and young smiled a universal welcome. Up sprang a score of rejoicing beaux, and our party was soon advantageously seated in the most select quarter of the hall.

Then another whisper, " *Who's that?* " began to circulate, as Agnes became the object of social curiosity. Hitherto we have seen Agnes only amongst her native hills, with a becoming background of stream and forest, of verdant wheat piercing the snow, of blue mountains meeting the sky in the distance. This may have made a difference; but alas, real beauty and conventional beauty are essentially different; the wild flower transplanted to a garden may bloom as sweetly as beside its parent brook, but how few will stop to view it. One thing, however, is certain, that Agnes was not the person to take the house by storm; had she appeared unsupported by Lel she might not have occasioned a remark. Any one in the least familiar with fashionable life must have observed that beauty is entirely an arbitrary thing. It is ordained and given out by the ruling clique that a certain debutante *is* beautiful — beautiful in spite of the stars and all creation. Whoever dares to dispute the edict is banished from the fairy land of the first circles; and thus the whole pack of timorous dependents and hoping outsiders swell the cry until a duped community is musical with her praise. Or should some fair planet be spied in a lower sphere, which threatens to eclipse the reigning star, the innocent orb is so pelted and persecuted by all the satellites of the skies that, shorn of her glory and her rays, she gladly descends beneath the horizon. Thus with Agnes; it required but a word from Lel to make her a paragon or a fright.

They were rather inclined to like her, but not willing to hazard an opinion without a full investigation of her claims. *Her* claims! Oh hollow, heartless mockery. She might have been as lovely as the masterpiece of Grecian art, she might have spent her life in deeds of glowing charity, she might have possessed every virtue which adorns the soul, every grace which encircles the mind, yet without the borrowed attributes of birth and fortune — of fortune at least — her claims would have fallen to the ground as unnoticed and unfruitful as the tears of poverty. Ay, more than this; the very possession of these virtues would have diminished her attraction; the narrow vision of the world below, deceived by the height of the column, mistakes elevation for littleness.

There sat our young rustic, just as if she were in the quiet parlor at Loretto, unchanged, undazzled, unawed by the splendor and bustle around her. She had thrown off Lel's nubia — she was averse to any ornament. In her novel position it was difficult to be natural. and at ease; few. are proof against open embarrass- ment or a still more palpable effort to conceal it. But Agnes was not thinking of the impression she was to make; she was merely amused and entertained by her first glance at *life*. She was still the same Agnes that sat before the wood-fire.

But Lel was in her element, a thousand times lovelier than she had ever been; her eyes flashed and sparkled like diamonds, and in all she said and did there was a grace and elegance of action never before revealed. Had Agnes been inclined to jealousy there was ample cause for it. Had Lel any defeat to revenge she would have been amply repaid by her present triumph.

"Ag," whispered Lel, "do you see that lady in the terrapin head-dress, with clusters of little eggs all over her hair, a dish for an epicure? There she sits, looking right straight at you. She is coming here in a moment to inquire *who you are*."

Agnes had already perceived the unpleasant stare of the lady alluded to, who was, in fact, rendered so conspicuous by nature and art that she might have been marked amongst a million. She had all the pride, mannerism, and affectation of wealth, without one symptom of good breeding. But her person, in spite of advancing age, was good ; and, on the whole, she was rather a favorable specimen of metallic aristocracy.

"You must secure her countenance," continued Lel; "she is one of the crowned heads, without whose interference you will be cast into exile."

"Ah, here comes Mrs. Hoity," muttered Mr. Almy to Melville, "for my niece's pedigree. I'll meet her." And, as the lady in question rose, like a queen from her throne, he boldly marched up the narrow avenue and intercepted her advance.

Now, Mrs. Hoity was a widow, and had been accused of more than one design on Mr. Almy's independence. However this may be, she professed the most devoted friendship for Lel, who, with exemplary filial humility, conceived herself solely indebted to her father for the honor.

"I wanted a word with your charming daughter, but I fear I shall not have time, as I see the orchestra are entering now. Pray tell me the name of that young stranger?"

"Miss Agnes Cleveland."

"Cleveland, Cleveland; who are the Clevelands?" inquired Mrs. Hoity.

"Very good people, I believe. Her father's dead."

"Ah! an heiress?" said the good lady, brightening up and casting an approving look on the debutante.

"Yes, her uncle has a snug little farm," replied Mr. Almy, gravely.

"A snug little farm!" echoed the other, with a dying smile. "Is that the sum and substance of her expectations?"

"No, no," pursued Mr. Almy, quietly, "she has very splendid expectations I believe, but the bequest is unfortunately so limited as to take effect only after her demise. The poor creature has everything to hope from her own death, nothing from that of her friends."

"Poor creature," sighed Mrs. Hoity, who actually thought that Mr. Almy was alluding to a peculiar will of some eccentric ancestor. "Is she related to you?"

"No; a mere connection, a country cousin of Lel's," added Mr. Almy, in a meaning whisper. And with an arrogant toss of the head, a smile to Melville and Lel, a cold stare at Agnes, this admirable widow resumed her seat.

"Have you scared off the cormorant?" whispered Melville.

"Did you not see how she sailed away at the first snuff of poverty and vitality?" answered Mr. Almy, bending his head to indulge a laugh.

"Father has killed you dead; Hoity's against you," said Lel.

"I thank him sincerely," replied Agnes, and the concert began with an overture by Lind-paintner.

"Pshaw!" muttered Lel, crushing the bill; "but we can talk if the music will let us. Let us fancy ourselves on the walls of Troy; I'll be your Helen and point out the heroes and heroines in the audience."

"Soon done," suggested Melville. "Point where you will, you'll find a Menelaus, or a Paris, or"——

"A Thersites," added Lel, giving him a most malicious look.

"Show me your friends first," said Agnes; "I do not care to see the others."

"My *friends?*" returned Lel, with an expression of blank surprise that convulsed her father and Melville with suppressed laughter, as, rising deliberately from her seat, she carefully inspected the room.

"Melville," she said at last, " you're taller than

I, will you take a look round for my friends! I can't find *one*."

Happily, the overture terminated at that instant, and the boisterous applause drowned the laugh they could no longer suppress.

After some mechanical waltzes of Lanner's came the duett from Jessonda.

"Now," said Lel, "we'll listen, if the talking will let us. You'll see one of my friends now."

Well might she call that exquisite morsel a friend. Ever beautiful and ever new, growing dearer and nobler by familiarity; whoever has heard it when the heart was heavy with sorrow, when the brain was weary with thought, when hope itself refused to cheer; whoever has heard it then will recognize it as a friend that whispered, "though the sky is overcast, the stars are still as sweetly shining in their old places."

But a group of young ladies and gentlemen near them kept up such an incessant clatter that Agnes could scarcely follow the music. An attempt was made to encore the piece, but it was vigorously hissed down for a new polka.

"Huzza for the nineteenth century!" cried Lel, her eyes flashing fire. "The mind may be marching onward, as they say, but it doesn't march to good music. This *is* awful."

"From the full house," observed Agnes, "I

was inclined to think this a music-mad community."

"A musician-mad community," interposed Melville.

"No, sir," resumed Lel, "a few come to listen, and a few weak creatures to exchange smiles with the performers, which ought not to make a rational man jealous; but the great majority come to see and to be seen."

"You are too hard," said Mr. Almy; "that's only a collateral pleasure."

"No, sir," replied Lel, "the principal attraction."

"Of course it is," said Melville; "it is not surprising that the first principle and ground-work of society should be the mainspring of a concert."

The C minor symphony shared the same fate, though insipidity itself was awed into silence by the sublime Adagio, which must always lay the spell of majesty on every human heart.

In the meantime it had spread all over the room that Agnes was only "*a country cousin;*" and when the concert was over, and Lel was surrounded by her *friends*, Agnes was as unnoticed and unmolested as if the seal of her vocation glowing on her forehead had been universally intelligible.

CHAPTER XI.

THERE may be many who no longer heed us because our unpretending story seems light and frivolous, because it is not sufficiently seasoned with moral reflections, because we have not thought proper to insert here and there a chapter of pointed theological discussion to balance the ingredients of love and folly, which must necessarily appear in a faithful reflection of everyday life. In all humility we entreat their patience. We do not claim profound sagacity or varied experience; but, after all, there may be something beneath the glittering surface of Loretto which even the good and wise need not utterly despise. At least we hope so. Our books of devotion, dictated by learned sanctity, are numerous and full of unction; our catechism is within reach of the poorest; our treatises on theology, our works of controversy, are able to carry conviction to every man's door. In all our churches the words of faith, hope, and charity are continually falling from anointed lips. Go listen there, ye who seek instruction, ye orphans who pine for a mother! Waste not a moment over these pages in the hope of a sentimental conversion! We only wish to show how the worm of the world may wither the fairest leaf on the tree of life; we only wish to caution the young, ay, and the old, against the siren songs they are singing around us, and to illustrate that there is nothing so little valued by society as the pleasures of religion, whilst nothing is less prized by religion than the pleasures of society.

Those who have accompanied us from Loretto to the city must have been attracted by love for the characters we have created, not by a relish excited by the commonplace incidents through which they have passed. It is but justice, then, to examine more minutely the mutual relations of our little group of friends, to explain some things which have already been obscurely hinted, to reveal others which may not be suspected.

Let us see what Lel thought that night. She was not given to jealousy, but for some time she had remarked a change in Melville's manner towards her. He was quite as attentive, quite as courteous, quite as agreeable; but he was no more the same to her, the indescribable *something* had passed away. But more than this, it seemed to her that Agnes alone called up in his face the very feeling she missed and no longer inspired. She feared that she loved him, but she would not believe it, and repelled the thought

as an unworthy suggestion. Still she was a
woman; she felt her superiority to Agnes in
the concert-room, and, perceiving, enjoyed it.
But now that she was alone, now that the momentary triumph was over, now that her better
nature had returned with darkness and silence,
she abhorred herself for her weakness. For the
first time in her life she had departed from her
standard of feminine pride and magnanimity;
she had raised her hand against a friend, her heart
was bleeding to think that she had merited the
Colonel's cruel suspicion.

As for Agnes, she thought of the beautiful music
she had heard, of Mr. Almy's kindness; she re-
flected long on Lel's misfortune in having so many
acquaintances without one friend, and then fell
asleep to dream of the Convent and her mother.

Mr. Almy, too, was thinking. He thought
that Lel might soon be married to Melville, in
whom she would have a protector worthy of her,
that then he might feel at liberty to contract
new obligations. He thought of the strength and
purity displayed in Agnes, of her perfect free-
dom from art and affectation, and became suddenly solicitous about his age and appearance. He
congratulated himself on having prevented the
threatened persecution of Mrs. Hoity and her
tribe, and resolved to keep the young visitor at

home, unmolested and to himself. Of course he acted from the most disinterested motives; for it would be a fearful thing if this inexperienced girl were entrapped by the wiles of some artful adventurer. In short, it was much more prudent to pursue a Castilian strictness in her regard and save himself from all responsibility.

Now, what thought Melville? We have not yet succeeded in clearly marking his character, which is more faintly drawn than that of his associates. It is not easy to distinguish him from the multitude of real and fictitious youths in whom young ladies see a hero or a sage. We have said enough, though, to intimate that Melville's charms were rather mental than physical, and that, but for his fortune, few in Lel's place would have loved him. There was a time when Lel was all in all to him, when he thought of no one else and hoped for no one else. But it had passed away, passed away in spite of him! He would give worlds to recall it, but it would not come, it would not come! He felt that he was doing her injustice, that he was unjustifiably abandoning a position he had taken, that he had gone too far to retract, that perhaps he had inspired an attachment more permanent than his own; but reason and resolve alike failed to make him retrace the lost ground over which his inclination once carried him so lightly. He had discovered Lel's noble nature, her firmness, her truth, and he revered her in spite of her foibles. She was worthier of love than any he had met. But he met Agnes! *Here* is something higher and holier, the realization of his fondest hopes! As he became better acquainted with her, Lel's imperfections were magnified into faults, until he wondered how he could have been fascinated by such a giddy, tattling creature. Thus he fluctuated between self-reproach and self-congratulation. At the concert he had seen Lel at every advantage, Agnes at every disadvantage, and though delighted by the brilliancy of the one, he was far more deeply moved by the noble repose of the other.

His reflections naturally resolved themselves into this one point : that he was still attached to Lel, but that his solemn duty to himself demanded that he should obey his mature judgment instead of blindly pursuing his juvenile inclinations. No very serious consequences could arise, because Lel was too generous not to forgive him, too light-hearted not to forget him. The matter must soon be decided — things had a hypocritical aspect as they stood — he hated deception and procrastination — at all events he would ask Agnes to ride with him to-morrow afternoon.

CHAPTER XII.

T was a bright, cold day; Melville and Agnes had gone out on horseback, Mr. Almy and Lel were spending the afternoon at home.

"Lel," said Mr. Almy, "I cannot tell you how much your cousin interests me. I have often followed little school-girls for squares to watch their faces. Sometimes I find amongst them one of those sweet young creatures wondering sadly at the world, on whom the bungling earth has not laid a touch to spoil the pure handiwork of heaven. I have wept as I followed them, to think that they *must* live, for they feel their exile. Agnes has one of these faces."

" She is as happy as the day's long," said Lel.

" Happier than you or I, perhaps," continued Mr. Almy; " but ask her whether she is not languishing for her home *there*, above the blue ether that bars the eagle's eye, and her answer will be ' Yes!' "

" I believe it would," returned Lel, mournfully.

" Are *we* the tempters who must destroy this beautiful hope, by substituting for it a clinging to the world, a false devotion to the artificial life *we* are leading?   Oh, Lel, Lel, when I think of the villains who approach you, who, steeped in iniquity to the lips, yet have the privilege of walking, talking, eating, and dancing with you, I despise myself for permitting it.   I had not the Christian firmness to prevent it; I lack the Roman heroism which should remedy it."

Lel had often determined to inform her father of Agnes' choice of life, and of the agony it caused the Colonel.   But in her heart, though she knew it not, she prayed that Agnes might adhere to her resolution and not permit the false glare of a *brilliant season* to melt her heroic promise.   She trembled at the responsibility of weaning the child of heaven from the breast from which it drew its first pure nourishment.   She feared that her father, out of earnest sympathy for the Colonel, might employ every art to win Agnes to the world.   This had kept her silent.   But her father was speaking as he had never spoken before; his whole frame was working as if he were giving vent to thoughts smothered for years.

"Father," she began, "forgive my concealing it; I should have told you at once, Agnes Cleveland is to be a nun."

"Of her own free choice?"

"Yes."

"Thank God!" cried Mr. Almy, and a light broke over his face, amid which Lel saw the expression he *ought to have.* "Thank God! But what is she doing here ?"

Lel hung her head.

"Does her mother oppose it ?"

"No ; her uncle does."

"The hoary old fool," thundered Mr. Almy, clenching his hand. "And he sent her here to be *reclaimed ?*" he added, bitterly.

"Yes," said Lel, "and I am his instrument."

"His instrument," repeated Mr. Almy, breathing deeply and drawing back from his daughter with involuntary disdain, "his instrument to seduce this vestal virgin from solitude and sanctity; his instrument to pervert the purest aspirations of the human soul; his instrument to deprive her of eternal joy for the sake of mortal life; and what a life! No, no, Lel, I will not believe it, you are not sunk so low."

"I am."

"Lel!" exclaimed Mr. Almy, grasping her arm, "I have been a cold, inconsiderate parent; I have but poorly played a father's part; I have neglected your soul, your immortal soul, because I loved the world more than heaven. I shall not speak of this now, not now. I love you, though, with all the love of which I am capable; you are dearer to me than all the earth. I would sacrifice fortune, health, life, to save you from one hour of the suffering that is my daily portion; but though I must love you thus to the day of my death, come what may, yet if you attempt by any influence, direct or indirect, to clip the wings of this beautiful soul now flying to its Maker's bosom, I shall cease to respect you."

"Oh, hear me, father. A good old man, with trembling hands and gray hair, knelt to me, and begged me, as I valued his peace and life, to prevent his child — for he loves her as his child — from taking this final step, without experience, without reflection, without trial."

"And is *she* to be sacrificed because *he* is old and foolish? Oh, Lel, the whisperings of God to a young heart undefiled by sin, and in constant communion with him, trusting, living, exulting in him alone, are worth ages of experience. Fervent piety is more than wisdom, without which reflection is nothing. And as for trial, are we to test her with acids, like a lump of gold, when our very touch is enough to change her nature?"

"I have not soiled her yet," said Lel, hurt at the insinuation; "but if you think me an unfit companion for her"——

"I have touched your pride, my sweet Lel," said Mr. Almy, drawing her to his side. "My dear daughter, you have fine impulses, glowing sentiments, correct notions of right and wrong, as the world goes ; you go to church pretty regularly, you say your prayers sometimes, you are a loving, dutiful child, but oh, Lel ! you are not what you might have been — what you might be had I done my duty, had I consulted your true interests, had I been true to your *mother's dying charge !* "

At these last words, uttered in a hoarse whisper, as if wrung by agony and remorse from his lips, the proud merchant staggered to a chair and buried his face in his hands, whilst Lel, pale and trembling, knelt before him.

"Enough, enough, the fault is mine !" murmured the father ; ask me no more, not one word more, as you value my repose. Will you believe it, my daughter, that often when you were attracting all eyes, and winning all hearts, I have wished, prayed, ay, a thousand times, prayed that you had died in your cradle before your feet had left your mother's chamber, before your lips had left your mother's breast. It was a wicked wish, but I wished it, I still wish it."

"Why ?"

"Because I have a conscience !" said Mr.

Almy, with bitter emphasis, and as he raised his eyes he encountered Gabriel's, who was smiling.

"You come and go like a ghost," continued Mr. Almy, addressing him; "I am glad you come now with a smile. What's the matter?"

"Tea is ready," whispered Gabriel, "and Miss Agnes and Mr. Melville are at the door."

We shall employ the time they are spending at the tea-table by relating what happened during the ride.

Melville did not feel exactly *happy* as he pranced so gayly beside Agnes; the future was not clear enough, his hopes were too far from fulfilment; yet he felt the charm of her presence, and was happier than he would have been anywhere else. At times, indeed, when Agnes gave full reign to the spirited creature that bore her, when, leaving the city behind, she flew into the country like an uncaged bird, or when, checking their horses they paced slowly along some wooded ridge, conversing as freely and fondly as if they had been friends from childhood, the sanguine young man flattered himself that the cold obstacles to his happiness were melting in the warm light of affection.

Away they went, as fleetly as happiness, through the suburbs, over the main road, passing from turnpike to turnpike by various winding lanes, new to Agnes, but familiar to her companion. The horses stopped of their own accord beside a little ice-bound brook, and then walked most leisurely. The road was shut in by hills and trees, and wound gradually from a hollow up to a high point of land, commanding a fine view of the city and the river beyond it. Melville smiled sadly; the intelligent animals were truer to the past than he. Yes, it was Lel's favorite ride! *There* had she been day after day with him; in spring, when the first flowers were blooming, when the loving leaves stretched forth their tender cheeks to the soft kisses of the south winds, and decked the reviving branches for wooing birds; in summer, when the little brook babbled against the heat, when thirsting doves came to drink and peck there, when the flocks and herds slumbered in the cool shade of noble oaks, when the bearded wheat and tasselled corn waved in green and gold; in autumn, when the mellow fruit glanced in beauty through the orchards, when every hill-top and every bottom glowed in gorgeous livery of a thousand dyes, as if the numberless leaves had caught and held fast the colors of the sunset clouds. The horses had always walked over that ground, and they respected it now.

No wonder then Melville looked grave, no wonder he hung his head. He knew the very stones; they preached to him most powerfully of mortal inconstancy; and as memory after memory returned, with a load of looks, words, and smiles, his heart smote him, and he felt like a traitor.

Agnes was not entirely blind, yet up to this instant she had never dreamed that Melville's attentions to her meant anything more than common friendship. To a pure, unsuspecting intelligence truth comes like inspiration. All at once it flashed upon her that Lel and Melville stood a little farther apart, and that she herself stood between them. And then, putting this and that together, she rapidly came to a conclusion from which she recoiled, unwilling to believe it. When Melville looked up, he met her calm, dark eye searching his very soul, and he blushed and trembled like a truant school-boy. His embarrassment confirmed her suspicion, and a sentiment resembling aversion arose in her mind. It was but a transient shadow, yet, had he not looked away, he could have seen, for once, that gentle face administering a cold rebuke.

"Can we return by that road?" she asked, urging her horse to a full gallop.

Melville muttered, "Yes."

"Let us take it, then; the sun will soon be down."

There were pretty cottages strung along each side of the road, some on the Barn, some on the Gothic, but most on the Vandal order, with here and there a dwelling of much pretension, its deformity rendered more conspicuous by its size. Agnes kept her companion busy telling her the names and history of the owners. His answers were not very entertaining or satisfactory, and the good people described could hardly have recognized themselves in the medley he made of them. In short, he so confounded their births, marriages, and deaths that it must have been the most wonderful population on the face of the earth. He still felt that calm, dark eye searching his very soul, and half his replies were at random, until, to his inexpressible relief, they reached the edge of the city, where she suspended her queries, to observe the dirty, cramped, dingy hovels through which they were passing.

"You must excuse my bringing you this very uninteresting route," said Melville. "I scarcely know where we are. However, it is easy to escape these palaces of the sovereign people."

"Excuse *me*," replied Agnes, surprised and pained by this heartless sneer; "excuse me if I find this the most interesting part of our ride."

Melville saw how far he had committed himself. Poor fellow! He was charitable or liberal to a fault; but, like all of us, in trying to appear to advantage, he only injured himself.

"Palaces they may be," she resumed, "of virtues that might put us, whom the poor need not envy, to the blush. Are these palaces ever visited by the rich, or are they avoided, as the Hindoo avoids a jungle which may conceal a lion?"

"Perhaps they do conceal a lion," said Melville.

"A very lean one, then," returned Agnes, glancing at the meagre forms that were flitting around them.

"Only the more desperate from hunger."

"And whose fault is that?" cried the young girl, with a flashing eye. "Were half the money that is squandered applied here the danger would be over."

"My fair friend is something of a Socialist."

"No," she retorted, with a smile. "If Christian charity were more in vogue Socialism, which only lives in its absence, would be out of fashion."

"It is their duty as Christians to bear and forbear."

"Most unquestionably. But if we neglect the duty of relieving are we to be surprised if they renounce the more difficult task of suffering?

A republic destitute of active Christian charity wants the first principle of life."

At this moment they were attracted by a little boy, who, darting through the door of an ill-looking shed, trotted along by their horses, holding his tiny hands up to Agnes with a gesture not to be mistaken. He could not have been more than ten years old; he was bareheaded, and his light, flaxen hair curled over his temples and cheeks. Though his clothes were tattered and old, yet his face and hands were scrupulously clean. Agnes was enchanted with him as he followed her, looking up with mild blue eyes from which his very soul appealed. Young as he was his smile was adorned with a touching mournfulness — it was like a star peering through a watery sky.

"What do you want, my boy?" said Agnes, stopping her horse.

"Help for my father," murmured the child, blushing and hanging his head.

"Perhaps his confusion should be construed into an admission of imposture," she whispered to Melville, and then continued, "What ails your father?"

"He has been very sick."

"Is he better?"

"Oh yes, much better. He is getting well."

"What does he want?"

The child was silent.

"Tell me!" said Agnes, in a tone of such heartfelt sympathy that the little fellow wondered, smiled, and wept.

"He never asks for anything," answered the boy, shaking his head, "he never asks for anything."

"Have you nothing to eat?" resumed Agnes.

"Yes, we have bread and meat enough for a week; but father won't eat it, and if he doesn't eat you know he must die." Here his tears flowed faster. "I thought — that if I could get money enough to buy him some nice things to-night he would be better in the morning. And when I saw you passing, something seemed to say to me, 'there goes a lady who will give you some oranges, and pineapples, and oysters.' For oh! you looked so good!" cried the artless child, looking into her eyes.

"Flattery, another proof of dishonesty. Shall we encourage this vagabond, Mr. Melville?" reaching down to pat the boy's head as she spoke.

"He attracts me strongly," whispered Melville, taking out his purse. "In spite of his light hair and blue eyes I think he slightly resembles you."

"What is your name, my son?" said Agnes.

"Clarence!"

"Have you no other name?"

"None."

"Where is your father?"

"In there," said the boy, pointing at the door from which he had issued.

"Can I see him?"

Again the round tears rolled over his soft cheeks, again his golden head inclined. Without a word he pressed her hand passionately to his lips, then gazed at her in mute reverence.

"You are not in earnest, Miss Agnes," cried Melville, as she was about to dismount.

"Indeed I am," and throwing him the reins, and giving her hand to the child, she sprang lightly from the saddle. Melville was instantly at her side.

"My dear Miss Cleveland," he said, "I implore you not to expose yourself to the close atmosphere of these cells, where you know not how many forms of disease may be lurking. Remain here; I will make an examination and see that the invalid is well nursed."

So saying, he beckoned a man to hold the horses, and stepped before her.

"We will go together," said Agnes, noticing Melville's concern for her and indifference to himself. But she could not be dissuaded by look, speech, or gesture; for not only did she long to begin her mission at the bedside of suffering poverty, not only did she think of bathing the invalid's temples and moistening his lips, but the man might be dying, an unshrived soul might be speeding to its last account!

Clarence led the way with his little hand fast in hers.

After ascending a narrow, crooked staircase, they entered a dismal chamber, uncarpeted and unpapered. They could scarcely see each other at first, for the room was badly lighted, and the broken windows were hung with blankets to nourish heat at the expense of light. The wretchedness of the scene, the imperfect ventilation, made Agnes dizzy, as, guided by Clarence, she approached a bed standing on a shabby piece of matting in one corner.

"He is sound asleep," whispered the boy; "he has not slept before for three days and nights."

"Give me a candle, if you have one," said Melville, drawing closer to the slumberer. Agnes shuddered — he was so still, his very breathing inaudible — it might be death!

Clarence hastily drew a match across the wall, and the last candle, revealing all the evidences of poverty and distress, deepened the wretchedness of the scene. Shading the light with his hand Melville bent over the sick man. Agnes saw a mass of black hair, a forehead white as marble; she saw the closed eye, the motionless lips, and clasping her hands knelt by the pillow; whilst Clarence, terrified at their deep silence, crept close to her side. She looked again,—did not the thin nostril move? did it not rise and fall regularly? She looked earnestly at Melville.

"He is living," he said at last; "his pulse is weak, but true; his breathing faint, but regular. My son," he continued, in a tone of unwonted tenderness, "your father will be much better when he wakes."

"When will he wake?" asked Clarence, with tearful eyes.

"Probably not before to-morrow."

"But if he should not wake then?"

"So much the better. Let him sleep on."

Agnes turned to embrace the boy, and to her surprise found the mysterious Gabriel amongst them.

"How did you find us out?" said Melville.

"I saw the horses at the door," whispered Gabriel.

"This atmosphere is enough to kill any one," resumed Melville, examining the windows.

Whilst he was improving the ventilation, Agnes moved about the room, like a sweet spirit, putting things in order. By her mere touch the rubbish around her seemed to lose its chaotic aspect. As we see a gentle, loving woman subduing the ruggedness of poverty by a smile, and reducing all to order, as if by the simple force of her presence, we are reminded of the Eternal Spirit that moved over the face of the waters, creating life and light and order by his breath alone.

Gabriel had taken Clarence on his knees. One of his peculiarities was a fondness for children which he could not control. He was never so happy as when he had them in his arms. And they all loved him, and would run to meet him and cling to him like young vines around the prop by which they curl towards the sky.

"Let us go, Miss Cleveland," said Melville.

"Leave him?" cried Agnes, in surprise.

"I will return and pass the night here; I have some skill in medicine. This is no place for you."

Agnes felt that she had done Melville injustice, and a smile of gratitude and approval shone on her face.

"But should he want a confessor?"

"Leave that to me," interposed Gabriel.

"The man is in no danger, I assure you," said Melville.

"I shall return in half an hour," whispered Gabriel to the child.

"Don't forget the oranges!" said Clarence. Gabriel smiled, and Agnes took the dear boy in her arms.

"When are you coming back?" asked Clarence, clinging to her.

"To-morrow morning early. Will you not go with me till then?"

Clarence pointed to his father, and Agnes kissed his clear, sunny forehead.

"Where do you sleep?" she said.

He pointed to a chair at the head of the bed.

Turning abruptly from him to hide her tears she left the room.

"Make no noise, my son," said Melville. He looked round for Gabriel, but Gabriel had already disappeared.

CHAPTER XIII.

AS we have seen, Gabriel reached the house a minute before the equestrians; his celerity was so marvellous that he might be called ubiquitous. At the tea-table Agnes acquainted Lel and her father with what had happened. Mr. Almy immediately ordered his carriage, and the girls busied themselves in gathering all the delicacies of the house into a goodly bundle. After this they selected a good bed and abundant covering for Clarence. All was put into the carriage in charge of Gabriel, who set out at once, Melville promising to follow soon.

The stranger was still asleep; Clarence was sitting by his bedside, thinking of the sweet looking lady who had been so kind to him. The poor boy had heard of angels, and in his solitude and sufferings he delighted to surround himself with those blessed creatures with whom he believed the air was peopled. They were his only playmates, and so vividly had he pictured them that he knew them by different forms and names, and loved to sing to them by day and call them to share his pillow when he was fortunate enough to have one. But Agnes seemed to him prettier than any of his invisible companions; and he was wondering whether some one of them had not stepped forth from the air to comfort and cheer him, in mortal shape, as Gabriel entered the room.

Without speaking, but smiling like another angel, this strange being spread the bed on the floor and made it up as nicely as a new chambermaid could have done. He then deposited the bundle in a corner, and took Clarence on his knee, drawing the chair away from the bed.

" You see I have not forgotten the oranges " he whispered, pulling some of the golden fruit from his pocket.

But Clarence was looking at the soft bed, the snow-white sheets, and spotless pillow-case.

" Is that for *me?* " he murmured.

" For you," replied Gabriel, kissing him, as the fair boy, leaning against his benefactor's breast, wept as if his heart would break. It was soon over; the tears of childhood are like April showers — for every drop, a flower, a smile.

" What is your father's name?" resumed Gabriel.

Clarence shook his head.

" Where were you born?"

"I do not know."

"Is your mother dead?"

"I never saw my mother," sighed the motherless boy.

" Where have you been living?"

"In England."

" All your life?"

"No," said the child after a pause, in which he seemed lost in thought. "I remember another land where the sun was warmer, where grapes and oranges grew on the hills. I remember travelling far and crossing the water, and feeling cold, and finding different fruits and different people. I could not understand what they said. Then we crossed the water again, and found it still colder, and everything different again — it was England."

"How long were you there?"

"Oh, a long time, three or four years."

"Have you always been poor?"

"Yes, always poor, but not so poor as now; father is sick so often."

"What does your father do for a living?"

"I don't know."

"Does he work?"

"I don't know. We travel about from city to city. He is with me nearly all day, puts me to bed at night, kisses me, tells me to go to sleep and bids me good-by. When I wake in the morning I find him lying beside me."

"You spoke of a warmer land," whispered Gabriel.

"Yes," said the boy, eagerly, his eyes glistening with tears, "a land where I wish to die. I should go to heaven if I died there, it seems to be so much nearer heaven than any other place on earth is."

"A land of hills and grapes! Are you a Catholic?"

Clarence opened his jacket and showed a silver medal hanging over his white breast.

"Your father too a Catholic?"

"Yes; he hears me my prayers and takes me with him to mass on Sundays."

During the conversation Gabriel had not forgotten to refresh the child from the bundle, and from his own deep, exhaustless pocket. Observing that the lids seemed to droop over those young eyes he forbore any further questioning. Soon the untasted apple dropped from the boy's hands — he had fallen asleep on Gabriel's bosom.

"Sleep soundly, sweet child!" but as he spoke Clarence woke, gazing round for his father.

"Undress, my boy, I will watch your father to-night."

"Will you?" said Clarence, kissing his hand and looking into his eyes. "Yes, you will! I will trust you. Wake me if he wants anything." So saying, he knelt and said his customary prayers with his head between Gabriel's knees; then timidly crept into his beautiful bed, and in an instant went sound asleep.

Gabriel knelt some time over his young charge, then rose and approached the sick man on tiptoe. The invalid for the first time moved, his brow contracted, and a slight spasm passed over his face. Then growing more and more restless, he drew his arms from under the thick quilt, his head began to rock, and finally he turned on his side with his face to the wall, as if oppressed by Gabriel's presence. Gabriel still stood over him, with an expression of peculiar solicitude and sadness. Suddenly he placed his hand over the stranger's heart; a deep groan answered the touch.

Melville's foot was on the staircase. Gabriel fell back from the bed, and as he did so the sick man returned to his former position and lay as quietly as before.

"The carriage is at the door," said Melville; "you had better return and report that all is going on well. I shall keep watch to-night."

Scarcely had the door closed on Gabriel than Melville, taking the candle from the hearth, approached the sufferer. With a trembling hand he pressed the matted hair back from the pale forehead.

" *Yes! it is he!* " Pale as the sleeper himself, he replaced the candle, and throwing himself in a chair, abandoned himself to the most harrowing thoughts. The scene itself, apart from association, was calculated to impress him deeply. There lay that beautiful boy, his cheek resting on his hand, a calm smile playing around his half-opened mouth; there lay the father as stern and still as death. The wind sighed mournfully through the broken panes and loose sashes, and rustled along the tattered hangings. Melville was too much excited to think collectedly, and the night seemed to him as endless as it does to a wounded soldier on the battle-field. The candle flickered in its socket, the formless shadows danced over the wall and ceiling. Twelve o'clock sounded, faintly tolled from afar off; the unwearying wheel of sin and pleasure is spinning around; his brain is spinning too; he feels tempted to rush from the room into the open air. At first, anxious to gratify his curiosity, he wished the sleeper to wake; its was too painful to watch that white, motionless form, alive, but giving no sign of life, a stranger, and yet perhaps something more than a friend. But now, though not easily daunted, he trembled lest he should awake, he prayed that he might sleep on till morning light. And yet he could not compose himself; in spite of his utmost efforts he paced up and down the room. He lit another candle brought by Gabriel; its clear light relieved the sepulchral aspect of the room, his spirits rose, he laughed at his childish dejection, and forced himself to hum over some of his favorite songs. His back was turned to the sleeper; there is a sudden start, *a motion in the bed!*

The song froze on his lips, a chill went through his heart. Turning, as if he had been wrenched round by a hand of iron, he saw the figure sitting upright, he saw two unnaturally large eyes fixed upon him ; it was as if a corpse had risen in the terror and majesty of death, as if the soul had returned from its last errand to drag the body after it.

Melville, unable to speak, stood gazing at the spectral stranger; it was a pause of fearful silence; the apparition was the first to speak.

" Who are you ?" sounded in a hollow voice.

" A friend," replied Melville, conquering his awe and advancing. " You must pardon this intrusion, it is kindly meant."

" Where is Clarence?" continued the other, searching the room with a rolling eye.

" Asleep at the foot of your bed."

" Poor fellow, he has a hard time of it. Raise me, let me see him."

Melville raised him in his arms until the boy was in view. The stranger, clasping his hands in mute thankfulness over his breast, sank back on his meagre pillow and wept; ay, that stern man wept, and his face became as soft as a woman's.

" Am I indebted to you for this?" he said, feebly pressing Melville's hand.

Melville shook his head and related the circumstances that led to his discovery, bringing Agnes forward in the beautiful relief she occupied in his own fancy.

"And who is she, this angel of mercy?"

Melville hesitated — he felt himself on dangerous ground — her name might excite an agitation fatal to the patient.

"My sister," he replied.

"And your name is"——

"Melville."

"Melville!" repeated the other, drawing his fingers across his forhead, "Melville."

"I think we have met before," and as the stranger searched his features, he began —

"*I am a wanderer!*"

"Indeed! — The music store in London? — Has that wretched, impious song served to connect me in sympathy with any human being. Oh, Mr. Melville, I have changed since then! I am still a wanderer, still a prodigal, still a villain, it may be, but that boy has bettered me, saved me. These are almost the first tears I have shed since childhood; but long accustomed to hardship and neglect, your sister's kindness at this moment makes me weep. I might scorn it, if rendered to me alone, but to that child — Bless her! bless her! and the unbidden tears coursed down his wasted cheeks.

"Poor boy," he resumed, "he leads a lonely life with me, and, yet I have seen him, for hours at a time, playing and talking with invisible companions — his angels, as he calls them. And who will say that those blessed spirits may not appear to a lonely, motherless boy, clad in baptismal innocence — that heaven may not minister to such a child, deprived of every earthly pleasure!"

Much as Melville wished to hear more he begged his patient, who was already exhausted, to compose himself to sleep. He had prudently brought some liquid nourishment, which he prevailed on him to take — there was no need of medicine; the man was well, and only required care. Whenever he attempted to speak Melville imposed silence by laying his fingers on his lips, saying, —

"We will converse to-morrow."

At last the wanderer's eyes closed — it was no longer a dull stagnation of the body, but a calm, refreshing sleep. Melville was comparatively happy; happy in the consciousness of doing good, happy that a new tie between him and Agnes was spun. But a task full of difficulty, requiring the greatest prudence and delicacy, was before him. Agnes had promised to return in the morning, and how to palm her off for his sister without awakening suspicion as strong as his own he knew not. Lel, too, would be sure to call her cousin by name; — one word might cost the invalid his life. It was necessary to make a confidant of Lel; thus he hoped, by practicing a harmless piece of deception, to obviate the danger. He felt that he was adopting the best course under the circumstances, and assured of the success of his plans the night passed swiftly by.

Gabriel came with the sun, bringing a glazier's box and a pair of window curtains; he had a knack of doing everything useful; and during the evening before, detecting the absence of three entire panes of glass, he determined to replace them himself.

Melville could not repress a smile.

"Do not go to work until he is wide awake," was his parting charge.

CHAPTER XIV.

ARLY the next morning Melville presented himself at Mr. Almy's door. The "royal merchant" was on his way to the counting-house, but the young ladies were expecting him with their bonnets on, ready to start for the scene of distress.

Lel stared at him in amazement.

"Remember — "*I am a wanderer!*"" They exchanged a look of intelligence, and separated.

"Do you think he will recover?" inquired Agnes.

"He has recovered," replied Melville; "all he wants is proper nourishment. His mind is a little disordered yet; for I noticed that he persisted in calling you my sister, and that my explanations, instead of correcting his unaccountable impression, only annoyed him. I think it better for you not to contradict him."

"Of course not," said Agnes. "But let us start."

"Do you mean to walk?" said Melville.

"Certainly," cried Lel. "I never ride when I can walk. If we walked longer, we'd wear longer, all of us."

Gabriel had wrought a wondrous change; the broken panes are restored, the old ones washed; instead of being obscured by dingy blankets and old clothes, the windows are now ornamented with neat green curtains; the floor is brushed and sprinkled with water; the chairs are symmetrically arranged; the trunk answers all the purposes of a sofa; Clarence's bed is prettily coiled up in one corner; the light fumes of a pastile are curling around the mantelpiece; there is an air of comfort and convalescence.

They found Gabriel washing his hands, the stranger propped up in bed by pillows; he was quite as much changed as the room. His long sleep and Gabriel's razor and linen had made him another man. He was playing with Clarence's long silken hair as they entered. Clarence, who had been listening eagerly, no sooner recognized Agnes than he flew to meet her like a young bird to its mother's beak.

Already there may have been noticed in the stranger's manner what the world calls breeding. Lel and Agnes were surprised to find every appearance of gentility in the sufferer whom they came to relieve. Melville and Lel both saw that his eye was fixed on Agnes, and that although he turned from her when replying to their inquiries about his health it required an effort to do so.

"I know not how to thank you, Miss Melville," he said, "this little boy must do it for me. I am perhaps incapable of gratitude, certainly unable to express it, having rarely been called upon to feel it."

Again they were surprised, not only at his language, but at the cultivated tone in which the words were uttered.

"I know not," he continued, "why you are so kind to a friendless wanderer, nor will I ask; the only reward I can promise is the prayers of my child."

"Reward enough for a Christian," said Agnes, patting the golden head that was leaning against her.

The stranger trembled ; her voice, her look, her motion, all reminded him too painfully of one whom she resembled. A deep flush passed over his pale cheek, his bosom heaved, his eyes glowed an instant with the unnatural light of delirium, and after an inward struggle, the shadow of fixed, familiar agony overspread his features. Melville trembled too; he feared lest they should discover the likeness which existed between them, and which was growing stronger every moment; he knew not how they could be blind to a resemblance so evident to him. Agnes ascribed his emotion to mental weakness, and fearing that their presence might retard his recovery, would have gone; but she felt herself attracted to him by a mysterious, overpowering influence. She longed to stay and hear more from the singular man in whom she took such a strange interest; his face, his voice, his manner touched her heart;

his evident refinement of person and feeling, his
miserable situation, inspired her with a wish to
communicate more freely with him — a wish that
was not altogether female curiosity.   It seemed
to her as if she could sit forever in the chair on
which Clarence used to sleep,— sit there forever
and listen to him, pray for him, nurse him, and
console him.

In vain they endeavored to recall, by indifferent questions, his former cheerfulness and com-
posure;   something had passed within his soul
which forbade it.   His eye no longer sought
Agnes; he seemed to avoid meeting hers; her
presence oppressed him.

"Let us be gone," whispered Lel.

Agnes reluctantly assented; but first taking
Clarence by the hand,—

"Trust me with your child until this afternoon," she said; "I will return him safe."

"Take him!" muttered the stranger; "take
him!" and with a look that startled her, he
pressed her hand to his lips.

"He is wandering," whispered Lel.

Clarence, blushing and hesitating, kissed his
father good-by, and taking his ragged hat, followed the young ladies into the street.

"Do not stay for me, Mr. Melville," said the
stranger after a long silence, "you have had no

sleep. I am but a poor chorus-singer, unworthy your attention."

"A chorus-singer in an opera?" inquired Melville.

"Yes."

"Where is your company?"

"They left me here unable to follow them. Once it would have been otherwise, but I am losing my voice and am no longer indispensable. They were right in leaving me."

"Can you obtain a support in this way?"

"Enough to live when I am well, enough to die when I am sick. I should be contented but for Clarence."

"I might," said Melville, respectfully, "I might possibly obtain for you more becoming and lucrative employment.

"No!" replied the stranger, with a touch of pride; my present life is my free choice, or I could change it myself."

There was a long pause.

"Do you not love your sister?" he resumed.

Melville could say "*yes*," with a clear conscience.

"Then never let her marry. Who was that bright young creature with her? she is made for the world."

"Miss Ellen Almy."

" The merchant's daughter ? " cried the other, shuddering. Melville, internally lamenting his imprudence, nodded affirmatively.

Again the Wanderer's face grew dark, and with agony keener than before.

"Leave me, Mr. Melville," he said; "think not harshly of my bluntness — but I must be alone, I must be alone. Come to-night, my friend, *come alone.*

Clarence and his fair protectors had reached the centre of the city. Agnes still held the boy by the hand, and Lel, though sensible of the singular appearance they were making, had not the heart to remonstrate with her cousin. Whom should they meet but the queenly Mrs. Hoity, sweeping the pavement with her satin skirts. Glancing at Agnes with ineffable disdain, she threw a side leer to Lel, and, when they had passed, indulged a hearty well-fed laugh, and raised her hands in majestic depreciation, exclaimed, " La me! so much for having country cousins. Were it not for Mr. Almy's sake I would positively decline dining with her to-day."

Unterrified by the apparition Agnes retained her hold until they reached a first-class clothing store. Clarence was placed in the shopkeeper's hands, and reappeared in a handsome dress. Dress makes many a fool pass current, and many a monster human. Few children in any station of life, though perfumed and petted from the cradle, could compare with Clarence in his new suit. Agnes did not see so great an alteration; but to Lel the transformation was little short of the miraculous. A handsome cloth cap completed his equipment.

He bore his honors meekly and naturally, appearing just as much at ease and quite as unaffected and self-forgetting as when adorning his rags.

"*He is made to be loved*," thought Lel. "*I wonder what his life will be!* Now, Clarence," she continued aloud, "you must go home with us and take a ride. After dinner you shall go home."

"*Home!*" sighed Agnes, opening the door and looking up at the clear blue skies.

Lel threw a cloak over the child's shoulders, and ordered the bill to be sent home.

CHAPTER XV.

R. ALMY had invited the *élite* of the city, Mrs. Hoity amongst others, to dine with Agnes. We need not describe the various courses, or enumerate the delicacies pro-

vided by epicurean waiters; things exacting so much time and health are better forgotten than remembered.

If Agnes was amazed at the profusion and elegance of the table, what shall we say of little Clarence, dazzled by the ·flashing decanters, and confounded by the majestic personages who appeared to be as much at home as wild pigeons in an oak-tree? Poor boy! his only hope was in Agnes.

Mrs. Hoity, upon whom Clarence had made a favorable impression, at length deigned to ask Agnes, next whom she sat, the charming urchin's name.

" I know not," was the reply, "but he is the ragged boy you passed this morning."

The proud widow's face turned to a deeper crimson, as she cooled her quivering lip in a glass of billowy champagne. It was insufferable to be in contact with such innate, unblushing vulgarity, and, had not respect for Mr. Almy restrained her, she would have left the table.

Lel had guessed the conversation, her eye sparkled with a wicked light, and quick as thought, she interposed, —

"It is only a habit he has of exchanging clothes with the first beggar he meets. He is the only son of Mr. Melville's sister, who, you should remember, married Count de la Roche, now dead."

" You could not deceive me, Miss Cleveland," resumed Mrs. Hoity, with a bitter accent. " I can always recognize *blood*."

Agnes, surprised at Lel's bold falsehood, paid no attention to her neighbor's remark; but Mr. Almy and Melville could scarcely contain themselves.

From that moment Clarence was Mrs. Hoity's idol; she overwhelmed him with her bland regards, throwing them across Agnes, who sat between them, in such a manner as to fan her cold by their rapid transmission. Agnes, unmindful of jest and dainty, thought of the poor wanderer on his dingy bed — thought of the future awaiting the beautiful boy at her side, who looked as though he were realizing the wildest pageant of the Arabian Nights.

She was glad when the ladies had permission to retire to the parlor, where they were to have some music from Lel. During the performance Mrs. Hoity, whose love for music was not excessive, employed herself in arranging Clarence's curls, smoothing and twisting them to greater symmetry. Once, with a praiseworthy gush of tenderness, she actually kissed him on the forehead. Clarence, whose soul was in the music, was annoyed and ashamed, especially as he wanted confidence in his patroness.

It was growing dark — the ladies were preparing to leave as Melville appeared.

"It is time for the boy to go home," he said.

"*We* will take him," said Lel.

"No," replied Melville, "his father begs to be excused until to-morrow; he was too much agitated this morning."

"His father!" muttered Mrs. Hoity to herself. "There is a mystery here; I have been deceived!" But, haughty as she was, she feared to resent an insult offered by the daughter of him she coveted, and smoothing her ruffled feathers as well as she could, she said good evening, without so much as a parting look to the young Count, who, a moment before, had been so high in her heart.

"Oh! thou glorious sample of humanity!" laughed Lel, when they were alone.

"I shall see you early to-morrow," said Agnes to Clarence.

The child looked up in her face as if they were parting forever. There is a presentiment of separation sometimes felt, without our being able to say why; we have no reason to fear, yet the event justifies the apprehension. It may be that a young, sensitive soul is influenced and forewarned by certain signs, of which the mind takes no notice, or, noticing, rejects. Thus it was with Clarence; as he beheld her pure, loving face shining on him, all he had ever known of a mother, he heard a voice saying, "Linger! Linger! *Years must pass before you meet again!*" ·

Agnes slipped into his pocket all that remained of her uncle's bounty; Lel increased the sum. Completely overcome, the boy seized their hands, and, kneeling before them, his uplifted face pale with emotion and wet with tears, said in a firm voice,—

"O, God, reward them well!"

It was ten o'clock; Melville had not yet returned. Lel and Agnes were playing chess; they could hear, now and then, the sound of revelry in the dining-room. At last it ceased, and Mr. Almy presented himself.

"What's become of Melville?" he cried. "Hang the fellow! why did he cut us just when we wanted him most? It is bad enough for you ladies to retreat, without enticing after you our best men, our picked soldiers, our tenth legion."

"Mr. Melville," said Lel, keeping her eye on the board, "went home with Clarence."

"Went to the devil!" muttered Mr. Almy, burying himself in a chair. "Oh, excuse me,

Miss Agnes," he added, seeing her astonishment; "his Satanic Majesty is a right respectable fellow after all."

Lel pressed her foot on her cousin's and bit her lip until it was white.

"The idea," continued Mr. Almy, "the bare idea of leaving such wine for the sake of a wandering brat! I could excuse him," waving his hand to Agnes, "if beauty had been the attraction; but to insult me in my own house out of charity — unnecessary, wanton, superfluous charity. Lel! light my cigar."

Agnes could see him without turning her face, So completely was her uncle lost in the object before her that she caught herself hoping that the real Mr. Almy would appear and expel the creature that aped him.

They went on playing, Lel keeping her eye riveted on the board. Before the game was over her father fell into a deep, heavy sleep.

"Come," whispered Lel, hearing his loud breathing and taking Agnes by the hand. They met Gabriel on the steps, but Lel paused not until she reached her room; then, locking the door, she threw herself into Agnes' arms, sobbing, "Oh, my father! my father!"

CHAPTER XV.

T break of day Gabriel repaired to the Wanderer's room; it was empty; the old trunk was no longer there; the beds were tenantless; Clarence and his mysterious father had disappeared! He played with the new green curtains, and looked through the clear new panes which he had inserted with so much care; it was work thrown away, love's labor lost.

He waited half an hour; they came not. He inquired below, but learned nothing. Murmuring a prayer, he glided from the room. Lel and Agnes were on the staircase.

"They have gone," he whispered, and passed them like a spirit.

Two weeks have flown without tidings of the Wanderer and his beautiful boy. They made diligent search, but in vain. Melville, the last who saw him, said that he left him sitting up; that his departure was entirely unexpected; that he had no intelligence of his movements. The stranger had made a deep impression upon Agnes; his pale face haunted her, and appeared in all her dreams. Clarence, too, had become so dear to her that she wept when she thought of

him.   She was heartily tired of the city, notwithstanding Lel's affection, Mr. Almy's kindness,
and Melville's devotion.   She longed for the solitude of Loretto; for her mother, the Colonel,
the convent.

Nor was Lel happier.   Alas, poor Lel! That
sweet singing-bird was drooping in the cage;
light-hearted as she was, it did not require a mi-
croscope to detect the worm of grief lurking beneath the gayly tinted rind of merriment.   She
saw that Melville loved Agnes; she could not
help seeing it.   Vanity of vanities! When the
eye that once sought us no longer seeks; when
the cheek that once glowed no longer blushes;
when the lips that once blessed no longer greet
us; when the hand that once trembled in ours is
cold and steady; when the heart we held, like a
juggler's ball, has eluded our grasp,—*then*, for-
sooth, we are ready to die; the world is desolate;
the skies are sunless; there is no life on the plain,
no light on the hills, and friendship itself is no
longer welcome, because our pride is humbled,
because a human being has *changed*, though above
us and around us the unchanging love of God is
beckoning on our souls to one who never disap-
points, to raptures that cannot pall.   Alas, poor
Lel!

Bitterly, bitterly did she feel it; yet she

blamed him not, and least of all did she blame Agnes, the innocent cause of her sorrow. The wounded pride that caused her pain helped her to conceal it, too. She had not to endure the shame, the degradation of being supplanted by an unworthy rival; his choice of Agnes displayed an elevation of soul that went far to excuse his fickleness. Yet the wound was deep; deeper than it seemed. She tried to heal it with music; but every chord was only musical of the past, of the blessed past, from which she was forever separated. How beautiful seemed that quiet convent which the Colonel detested! Had religion a balm which even music could not bestow?

Melville was in a tumult; he had had a conversation with *the Wanderer* which disturbed him; Mr. Almy, at Agnes' request, had informed him of her intention to be a nun; she meant to return to Loretto in a week—her return would confirm her resolution; it was necessary, though their acquaintance had been brief, to come to the point at once.

The moment at length arrived when he might speak; he and Agnes were alone together in the parlor, thanks to Lel, who, with feminine delicacy, guessing and respecting his purpose, had prevailed upon her father to take a long walk.

It is hard to say whether these *very particular* interviews are more embarrassing to the narrator or the parties themselves.

Melville, of course, like a popular orator, began as far off from the real question as possible. However, after some preliminary meandering, he innocently said, —

" You have some idea of entering a convent?"

" Who has told you so?" replied Agnes, smiling.

"Mr. Almy. Is it so?"

" Not exactly so," pursued Agnes quietly; "'some idea of entering a convent' does not express my deliberate, unalterable resolution to do it."

Melville was frozen by her firm, unrelenting tone, but, summoning all his courage, he proceeded : —

" Do you think, Miss Cleveland, that, instead of leading a life useful to your fellow-creatures, you are justified in immuring yourself in a cell, where you can be of no service to them ? "

" What do you mean by ' useful to my fellow-creatures?'" returned Agnes. " Is it by living as your friends in this city do?"

" By taking your proper place in society to correct and adorn it."

"You do me too much honor," said Agnes, "But if, instead of correcting and adorning it, I feel certain that it will infect and deform me?"

"How can you be certain of this?"

"By the practice of my religion."

"Are there not some, at least, in the world who by their virtues diminish its vices?"

"Certainly," she said; "but I am not one of the number."

"How do you know that you are not?"

"By the practice of my religion."

He could not, for the life of him, help wishing her a heathen.

"Does the practice of your religion permit you to rob us of your good example?"

"If the example I set in giving myself entirely to God has no effect, I do not see how I could well be a pattern."

"But *do* you give yourself entirely to God when you sacrifice man?"

"*I* sacrifice man! Why Mr. Melville, a great statesman dies and is forgotten in three days; cannot I enter a convent without slaughtering a hecatomb?"

"But if all thought as you do what would it end in?"

"Heaven!" cried Agnes, brightening as she spoke. "It appears to me that you people of the world are very hard upon those who wish to consecrate themselves to God, while you exact no account from the vast majorities who belong neither to God nor man — I mean society. I tell you, Mr. Melville, that the motives which keep people *in* the world are infinitely inferior to those which take them *out* of it into the cloister. But to return: we are not all missionaries; it is enough to save ourselves without saving our neighbors too. Our own salvation is the first point; we cannot attain that without praying for others, and prayers, believe me, do good. But if you really want profitable instruction, instead of idle discussion, study Kempis on nature and grace."

Melville shook his head sadly.

"So much for a life of perpetual contemplation and prayer," continued Agnes; "it is surely a holy one; nor do I see why I cannot embrace it because the world don't choose to behave themselves. If I felt a special mission to reform them it would be otherwise. But have you ever heard of a Sister of Charity?"

Melville smiled.

"You have heard of their prompt fearlessness, when pestilence scares away your worldlings; you have heard of their numberless acts of unre-warded benevolence; but you never suspected that these virtues which attract attention and applause are insignificant when contrasted with the heroism they display by voluntary perseverance in obedience, year after year, until a sweet death repays them at last. If such a life is not useful to man, pray tell me what is? Most of the orders in our church are what you would call utilitarian. Have you any objection to my becoming a Sister of Charity?"

"I can never believe," replied Melville, "that heaven exacts such a sacrifice from any of us."

"Heaven *always* exacts a sacrifice — the sacrifice of the body."

"But not of the soul."

"Of the soul!" said Agnes, clasping her hands. "Do I sacrifice my soul when, by denying it every natural gratification, I flood it with the joys of grace?"

"Then you enter a convent for the sake of pleasure?"

"For the pleasure of living for God and doing his holy will. You have changed your ground."

"*Must* we lose you then?" pursued Melville, forsaking argument for entreaty. "You will make me hate your religion!"

"I ought to make you love it!"

"And, for your sake, I hoped and still hope to love it," said Melville, seizing at the word.

"Oh, Agnes," he continued fervently, "would to heaven I had known your determination sooner, or could change it now! I love you too well to lose you thus! From the moment"——

"Stop, sir! Had I suspected your love you *should* have known it sooner; but I never dreamed of it until our horses stopped at the brook the evening we found the stranger. Since then I have done all in my power to discourage an affection so sudden, so hopeless, so unjust."

"So unjust?" echoed Melville, half petrified.

"Ay, so *unjust*," repeated Agnes. "Did you not once love Ellen Almy?"

Melville hung his head.

"Did you not let her see it?"

He was silent.

"Did you ever declare your love?"

"Never!" cried Melville, grasping at a ray of hope. "I was always deterred by her levity and apparent indifference."

"I could not suppose you base enough," resumed Agnes, "to break a solemn declaration, to which the world attaches so much importance; it would cost you your standing as a man of honor. But tell me, Mr. Melville, when eyes and actions have attested an existing love, and inspired a return, are we at liberty to break the bond because there is no verbal compact? It is unmanly and ungenerous, to say the least."

"She cannot love me!" said Melville, stung to the quick; "she is too reckless, too giddy, too fickle to love any one longer than an hour."

"You do her bitter injustice," replied Agnes, rising; "she is a woman whose love would enrich a throne! A light manner may accompany a strong, true heart, just as exterior dignity may hide a weak one. And you know it; you know that there is not beneath the sun a better, a purer, lovelier, loftier nature than Ellen Almy's."

"Is your resolution unalterable?" said Melville, with an accent of despair.

"Unalterable!" and wishing him good evening, she left him in no very enviable condition.

CHAPTER. XVII.

AM not surprised at it," said Mr. Almy to Lel, during their walk, dwelling upon a topic he had forced upon her attention, "I am not surprised at it, nor do I think the less of him. On the contrary, I honor him for it. True love of what is really lovely is

so rare that in any shape, almost, it is highly commendable. The bulk of mortals are blind to the infinite beauty and majesty of God; so the more nearly we approach him the more we are despised. In all matches where interest is out of question chance and vanity predominate; and from the way in which innocence is seen to cleave to depravity, I am inclined to think there is a sneaking fondness for the devil in the best of us. No. no; I like Melville for this, it is a beautiful trait."

"Do you think she will accept him?" asked Lel.

"Accept him?" said her father; "she cares no more for him than I do for the glorious Mrs. Hoity. That girl's aim is above this world; she cannot live for man without renouncing a manifest vocation, and renouncing that, she would never be able to make a husband happy. Some are made to marry and some are not. I can't exactly express my meaning, but there's something in what I've said, depend upon it."

"I think she would be happier with him than in a convent," suggested Lel, fully believing it.

"Nonsense! they would both be miserable. I'm somewhere in the neighborhood of a hidden truth, but can't strike it fairly. Agnes married!—Ha!" and he laughed—"It's perfectly ridiculous! Why, she would lose her lustre like a cloud when the sun, that clothed it in gold and purple, has set. Now she is as much your superior as can be; though if any one were silly enough to put you both in a book, you would be the favorite by all odds. Yet, let her marry, even I should cease to love her, unless perhaps I were obliged to."

"I don't understand you at all," said Lel, repeating his jumbled harangue.

"I don't expect to be understood," returned Mr. Almy. "Oh, it's a fine trait in Melville, to love her! I thought the fellow an irreclaimable infidel, but I've hopes of him now; I might even consent to let him have you."

"Would you ever have refused?"

"Certainly, and most decidedly, unless I saw you were breaking your heart about it, which is too unfashionable for you to be guilty of. Why, the man's not a Christian."

"Are you?" inquired Lel, with mock gravity.

Mr. Almy, pressing her arm, earnestly replied, "Your *mother* was!"

Lel found Agnes in her room; the meeting was a painful one, but Agnes determined to make the best of it.

"What do you think, Lel? Mr. Melville has been trying to persuade me not to enter the convent."

"Did he succeed?"

"Not quite. After a long argument he told me that he loved me."

"Was not that convincing?" said Lel, avoiding her cousin's gaze.

"So far from it," replied Agnes, "that I fear I treated him rudely."

"I hope not; indeed he does not deserve it. He would make you happy."

"No, my dearest Lel," said Agnes, embracing her, "he would make *you* happy, not me."

They had never before alluded to the subject, but they understood each other as well as if they had spoken volumes.

Lel's eyes, already full, ran over — Agnes had divined her secret — it was of no avail to conceal her grief. We must let those sacred moments pass in silence.

"But, when you leave me, Agnes? Tell me you will not leave me — I cannot live without you!"

"Can you not return to Loretto with me?"

"No, no," said Lel; "I shall not leave my father again."

"You once asked me to explain your father's

face," returned Agnes, anxious to divert her mind; "I think I can satisfy you now. People are apt to acquire that worst of all curses, *a false conscience.* When we get this it answers all the purposes of innocence, and makes us attractive; but when, though sinning on, we preserve a true conscience, self-condemnation makes us repulsive; wanting confidence in ourselves we cannot obtain it from others. All your father needs to render him benevolent-looking is a false conscience."

"Yes, yes," said Lel, interested in anything relating to her father, "You are right. Mignon dies and Felix stays with us — now, I understand Wilhelm Meister. Have you read it? Oh, Agnes, don't be a nun! You have mind enough for anything. If you'll only marry Melville, so that I may have you near me, that I may run in and see you when I please, plague you, play for you, sing for you, I shall be happy. I'll love some one else, and marry just to keep you from being jealous, and then " — but her eyes again ran over as she spoke. "Won't you stay with me a week longer?" she resumed.

"Make up your mind to return with me," replied Agnes.

"No, no, I'll stay here; I shall have enough to laugh at in Mrs. Hoity, enough to work at in

Listz, enough to idle at in new poems, and enough to sleep at in the congressional debates. I understand my father now — blessings on your insight! — and come what may, I care not. Must I change my nature because another has changed his mind; must I imitate his fickleness by playing false to myself? Never while my name's Lel!"

Words, words, words! — the eagle soars with the arrow in its side — the shaft must be in awhile before the wing closes.

Now for Melville. If we follow him to his rooms we shall find him surrounded by comfort and elegance. His mantelpiece is adorned with choice castings brought from abroad, the walls are gemmed with rare paintings and engravings, selected with judgment and taste. But there he sits dejectedly before his grate; he tried to read — absurd; he tried to write — impossible; he tried to caress a noble Newfoundland dog, who appeared to have some sympathy for his master — contemptible. In the blank despair of the first shock he felt like poor Gloster, as if another Regan had plucked his eyes out, as if curse of love had doomed him to wander, like Vathek, with his hand forever upon his heart.

Too well remembering her manner, it seemed to him cold, disdainful, masculine; — and flattering himself that he had been wasting his sunlight on an obstinate icicle, he suffered from that worst arrow 'in Cupid's quiver — devotion to an unworthy object. But, before midnight, his senses partially returned. Had he not been unjust to Lel, — had he not thus merited the rebuke so unmercifully administered by Agnes — had she not evinced her superiority of mind and feeling by detecting and reproving his inconstancy? But *there* was the rub! Might not the knowledge of this — might not the suspicion of a lingering affection for Lel prevent her love? Alas! what excuse will not the human heart invent to shield itself from admitting that its want of success is its own fault! The windings, turnings, twistings of disappointed love are too pitifully comic for analysis. A woman, in this condition, invites a tear; a man, a laugh.

Melville was not imaginative; his affections were always guided by his reason; yet Shakspeare himself could not have suffered more then he did then. A warm fancy is often mistaken for a warm heart, because it has all the language of sorrow when feeling is dumb.

We shall try not to laugh at him, since he

grew humbler towards morning. How could she love me, he said, — what have I to attract her besides wealth, that gilded bait which a noble nature scorns? I have no accomplishments, no social qualities, no beauty, no grace — I never have been loved — never will be — never will attempt to be again! If anybody wants me they must court me, propose, run off with me, and marry me; otherwise, I and my dog forever! And he said all this as seriously as could be, with a burning, beating forehead and a cold hand.

Poor Melville? in enumerating his deficiencies he omitted, "I have no religion;" he did not consider the absence of this a blemish; and how few do in all the written and unwritten tragedy and comedy of human love.

CHAPTER XVIII.

MELVILLE felt like an orphan — worse than an orphan. Sensitive creature, he had not the courage to present himself at Mr. Almy's — his temerity and fickleness had deprived him of the society of that delightful house, his only home. To relieve his spiritual desolation he was tempted to seek forgetfulness in the sparkling Lethe of dissipation. But Gabriel, the ever-present and all-seeing Gabriel, failed not to visit him in these moments of despondency, and whisper words of strength and consolation. This meek, benevolent being was the only link between him and the charming family from which he was forever exiled. Some words that fell from the Wanderer kept perpetually recurring to him — *"Do you love your sister Agnes? then never let her marry."* What could the man mean? Did he mean anything? When tired with vain attempts to solve this difficult problem he was naturally led to comtemplate Lel, *the bright young creature who was made for the world,"* and his meditations generally terminated with this remarkable wish, —

" *Oh, if Lel had only a little more of Agnes in her!* "

One morning, as he was trying hard to read a newspaper, Mr. Almy presented himself, and, slapping him on the shoulder as cordially as ever, said : —

" Melville, what in the deuce do you mean by treating me in this way? We are to have some music to-night, the German will be there, and if you don't come beware of me in future."

Melville, greatly relieved, thanked him, promising punctual attendance, and the generous merchant departed.

"What a happy man!" sighed Melville; "he does not seem to have a care on his mind."

At that moment there were cares enough on Mr. Almy's mind to break down three Melvilles, unschooled in affliction.

"Yes, I will go!" mused Melville, in suppressed heroics; "I will go, if only to show that I am calm; I will have no eyes to count the spasms of my mouth, or note the changes of my cheek, and least of all shall Agnes behold the ruin she has made!" So saying, he finished his breakfast with something of an appetite.

"Do you mean to have a ball to-night?" inquired Agnes of Lel, as they were sitting together. "Tell me frankly, for if you do, I shall not be present."

"A ball! Nonsense," replied Lel; "it will be nothing more than one of our old Thursday evenings, with a supper. Father made me put '*musicale*' in every invitation, that the ladies might dress decently on your account."

A waiter interrupted them with letters from the Colonel. They were models of brevity, if nothing else: —

"DEAR AGNES,—All well, including Charlie. We don't miss you more than we did when you were at the convent. Respects to Almy. Ever yours, etc."

"DEAR LEL, — How goes the game? Are not your knights an overmatch for her bishops?"

The cousins looked up at each other and smiled, without exchanging letters or making any comments on their contents.

"Do you think Melville will come?" resumed Lel.

"Of course he will," replied the other.

"Now, mark me, Agnes; if I betray what I feel by the slightest symptom I promise to enter the convent with you. The storm in my heart, the thunder on my brow, the lightning in my eye, the rain on my cheeks, the gale on my lips, shall all be covered by a cloudless sky and sunshine without a shadow; and if you never saw a woman who looked as though she knew not grief, nor ever could know it, you shall see her counterfeit this evening in me!"

CHAPTER XIX.

THE parlors are lighted, the lamps are glowing. Lel is in pink, Agnes in white, Mr. Almy in black. The guests are coming, the rustling of satin and silk begins, the rooms are filling. Close by the open piano, toying with his violoncello, known but unnoticed, sat a middle-aged man, with true German impenetrability. Hard-featured, thick-set, apathetic, he looked like anything but a genius. Yet, to Agnes, Mr. Almy excepted, he was the most interesting person in the room.

"Shall we commence?" said Lel to the musicians, as she took her seat. A moment's pause, and away they went at the first movement of Mendélssohn's first trio. Rapid and subtle as light, the earnest melody leaps from instrument to instrument, while unflagging and unceasing the motherly piano underlies, connects, and blends the whole. But when they reached the Adagio a light overspread the German's broad face, his soul shone through its unworthy casing, the living notes seemed to ooze, like Bob Acre's courage, through his fingers' ends, his hand was endowed with tones more eloquent than speech. Who that saw him then anticipated such a close to so much genius — so sudden, so piteous, so terrible! Like many before him of equal gifts, he has gone ignobly and unrewarded to the grave — his life wasted, his hopes blasted, his soul neglected. Like many who will follow him, he has withered like an uprooted flower in the hand that only prized it a moment, and cast it off as soon as it began to droop. How few that loved to hear him strove to help him!. 'Twas his own fault — sleep soundly, sweet world, sleep soundly!

Yet never to be forgotten by some, are those rare moments that come, like wind from another clime, laden with choicer perfumes than ours! *They* will sometimes think of the master who sleeps far away from his fatherland, and sometimes pray for him. No stone marks his grave, not a tear was shed for him! It is singular that those who neglected him in life do not honor him in ashes; for if he did not live like a genius surely he died like one.

Again the spell of music was laid on Melville. He could not remove his eyes from Lel, who appeared to float with the magic sounds, as if she were the muse who had first inspired the beauty she was reproducing. Who can say what passed in his heart, what years were revived and re-enjoyed in those delightful and all-powerful minutes? Was there not *a little more of Agnes* in her than he had lately imagined? During the playful Scherzo a childlike smile hovered around her mouth, and during the fairy-like finale her eyes swam in dreamy lustre.

It was over; the rooms were full. Mr. Almy's friends are there — sober-looking men, with the weight of the world on their shoulders; their faces screwed up by habit, rather than marked by thought, with calculation lurking in the spotless folds of their white cravats. Lel's *friends* are there; fair young girls absorbed in their first impressions, whose brains seem to have been consumed in nourishing their cultivated hair; others, a *little* older, who rejoice in candle-light as a blessed invention to contradict the lies which the garish sun might tell of them; others decidedly old, yet firmly persuaded that dignity is superior to grace, amongst whom —let her not be forgotten —towered the immortal Mrs. Hoity.

"If these people," thought Agnes, "come here for music's sake I am much mistaken."

She was not mistaken. During the first piece they had given signs of enjoyment, if not of appreciation; but their patience gave out in the second Trio, which was too elaborate to afford them even a pretext for a smile. They could have danced for joy when it died off like a shabby friend or a poor lover. But did they dance?

Music of another kind was heard —music from bells, and clarionets, and flutes, and fiddles. How infinitely inferior! how much more grateful!

Like veterans answering the trumpeter, they fell into order; two quadrilles were instantaneously formed. Agnes, professing her inability to dance, retreats behind Mr. Almy, and enters

into conversation with the German. Lel kept
her promise well. Light and graceful as a fawn,
she glided through every figure; her face beaming, her eye sparkling, her arms waving. The
life and 'soul of the room, her clear laugh rang
like morning music on the hill-tops, when shep-
herds and shepherdesses are greeting the rising
sun. Not once did she falter; not once did she
droop; not once did she betray, by over-acting,
that beneath all this there was a silent sorrow.

But Melville, poor Melville, was not so successful. He could have stood anything but Lel's
merriment and indifference, but that broke him
down. "I knew she never loved me," he muttered, "but now she despises me!" Dark as
death, he moved over to the German, and through
him renewed his acquaintance with Agnes. But
Agnes was icy cold and slid off with Mr. Almy.
A desperate purpose crossed him, to break abruptly from the company — but this was too much
like Sylvius, and he was too much of a gentleman.
Then he resolved to devote himself to the pret-
tiest and richest girl in the room; but his heart
failed him. He couldn't talk; he could only look
at Lel, lamenting that she was just as fickle as
himself.

All is bright, all is beautiful, all is joy, all is
gladness! It is so dreamlike, so enchanting, so

alluring, so ensnaring! The world is doing its best; all its ornaments are on; all its rags are off! Eyes are glancing; cheeks are glowing; whispers flowing! The walls shut out earth; the ceiling shuts out heaven!

Agnes, Agnes, beware! A fatal stream is rushing by thee; its banks are blooming, its waters sweet! Beware! beware! Thy feet are in it; it will sweep thee out to a stormy sea! May not the ermine perish in the snow? May not the camel falter in the desert?

For a time she remained alone with Mr. Almy. It took them hours to see her beauty, but they gathered round her at last, and she stood the centre of a brilliant circle. Excited by conversation, her dark eye flashes, the rose mantles proudly in her cheek. Introduction follows introduction, compliment follows compliment. Her praises are sounding through the room, in those terrible whispers which are meant to be heard. She is dealing with men and women of wit and information; boys and girls are listening in respectful silence. *Then*, 'all she had read and thought came thrilling to her tongue, and gushed forth like the first waters from a long sealed fountain.

Lel trembled; she scarcely recognized the timid lily of Loretto in the splendid woman before her. Where was Agnes? Was she dead; was the chrysalis soaring on these golden wings? Was she exchanging her immortal pinions for these fleeting feathers of an hour?

Who could have guessed that all this was sleeping in Agnes, till the breath of admiration should awake it? Had *she* not known it? Had she not feared it? Yes! yes! But was she not enjoying it? Does not the eaglet exult when, trusting to its untried wing, it finds the air its own?

"I knew it was in her," said Mr. Almy to himself; "I knew there was burning gold imprisoned within that cold marble."

The music is sounding; Mr. Almy, offering his arm to Agnes, leads the way to the supper-room.

All is bright, all is beautiful, all is joyous! The table is as luscious as a Moslem's paradise!

There are ices to cool the mouth and wines to fire the brain! Away with the past! Away with to-morrow! The blessings of a lifetime are crowded in to-night. Oh! how dream-like; oh! how dove-like; oh! how winning!

Agnes is still in the ascendant; she wields the sceptre of empire, as if she were born to it. Emulous youths are striving for her smiles and treasuring her words; transported merchants are unbending! in the buzz of admiration even jealousy is mute.

"Oh," thought Lel, "could the Colonel see her now, how his old heart would leap for joy! Here is *the woman of the world* he wishes."

Mothers are asking her expectations, daughters her age. Sons are speculating on the state of her affections. Again the foaming wine kisses the rim of her glass, again she raises it! The flashing eye, the arched lip, the quivering nostril, the haughty brow, were all there!

"Look," whispered Melville to Lel, "behold the Wanderer!"

The likeness was painful; but as they looked it vanished.

The glass almost fell from her hand. Alone in a corner stands Gabriel, unnoticed until then. No longer smiling, his brow is sternly knit, though from his steady eye, which pierced her very soul, tears of anguish were falling fast. Brushing his tears away, he quietly approached Mr. Almy and drew him into the passage.

What has happened to Agnes? The queen of the room is mute and sad. As the thunderbolt shivers a blossoming tree, Gabriel's look had struck her to the ground. All she wanted from earth was a place to lie down and weep, alone, the rest of her life. But they are crowding her

still, with a thousand questions, a thousand so-
licitations, a thousand persecutions. Where was
the light that dazzled her? It is but a dismal
flame that blisters! Where was the music that
enchanted her? It is but sharp discord that
offends.

And now from the supper-room troop the
gentlemen, in wine refulgent. The scene is
changing fast from mirth to madness, from folly
to revelry, from a parlor to a bar-room.

Sickened, shamed, and dispirited, Agnes rose
to retire, but met Mr. Almy. White as her
dress, he grasped her arm,—

"You are not going, Agnes?"

"Yes."

"Stay, for God's sake!" and he mingled with
the crowd. She watched him anxiously. His
laugh still rang, but it was forced and hollow;
his jests were wild and bitter, and when he
pledged his fellow merchants, he drank so deeply
and stared so strangely that they knew not what
to make of him.

Lel, whose heart was in her mouth, ventured
to ask him what the matter was, for in spite of
his utmost efforts to conceal his agitation it was
too apparent.

"Nothing, nothing!" was his only answer, as
he flitted like a spectre from group to group,

bidding them to enjoy themselves, in tones inspiring anything but happiness.

The company have gone, the last lingering drunkard has staggered off. Mr. Almy is lying on the sofa, Lel and Agnes are kneeling beside him.

"Speak! speak! I can endure the worst!" cried Lel, raising him in her arms.

"So can I!" said Mr. Almy, starting up and pacing the room. "So can I endure the worst!"

He stood still and clutched the back of a chair convulsively, the veins swelled in his temples, a groan burst from his lips, his head fell on his breast.

"Father!" screamed Lel, "in God's name, speak, or I shall die!"

He seemed not to hear her; she repeated it again and again. He placed his hands on her shoulder, he threw back her hair from her face, he fixed his eyes on hers. There they remained gazing at each other, the one in terror, the other in vacant anguish. At last his tears rained down upon her uplifted face, and falling on her neck, he cried, —

"*My daughter, I am a ruined merchant; I must fail to-morrow!*"

CHAPTER XX.

RIGHT rose the sun of the morrow. The sun that so often sympathizes with us showed no concern then. Almy has failed, was in every mouth. *Impossible*, said some; *strange*, said others; *very likely*, said the wise ones, shrugging their shoulders with a knowing look. Oh! when a house is falling how the world scampers off. "Away! away! Beware of the ruins!" Stand off, ye coward herd, the tiles are coming down, remember Pyrrhus! Yet there are a few, be it said for the honor of human nature, who step forward to solace with affection, if not to prop with courage. There are some who rejoice in having an opportunity to prove their magnanimity. They come with sweet words and bland manners, to fling some verdure around the ruins, and pardon the proud ingratitude which a reverse of fortune so often produces.

Melville could not believe it. Yet he had noticed Mr. Almy's manner, his counterfeit gayety, his pallor, his unnatural laugh. Could it be? He flew to learn the truth from the lips of his friend.

Mr. Almy was in bed breathing heavily, his pulse bounding like a lute-string. The report was true, for Lel and Agnes were in tears. The royal merchant held out his hand to Melville, who pressed it fervently. Not a word was said, until Melville whispered,—

"Why did you not tell me last night?"

"It was useless," and the merchant shook his head. "The crash in England has done it. A hundred thousand will not cover me!"

"Oh that you had told me last night!" repeated Melville, burying his face in his hands.

A generous purpose leaps forth like a meteor from the sky. Melville rose from his seat and silently pressed Lel's hand in his. Moments, moments, how ye govern years! He gazed awhile on her pale, tearful face, then hurried from the room.

He hastened to the counting-house; the clerks were in consternation; heavy payments to be met that morning, and the master of the house in bed. Melville seated himself at the desk; it was like a rush on a bank, but he met it. He entered the store a rich man and left it penniless. But no one else had lost a cent; and, as he retraced his steps, he felt that he had a right to look Lel once more in the face, and he would not have taken millions for the feeling.

Imagine Mr. Almy's surprise when his head clerk appeared with a balance-sheet, showing a trifle over all his liabilities. But alas! his notes had been protested; his credit, that ægis of mercantile honor, was gone; his house was tainted.

"Go on with the house," he muttered. What would he not have given to rise and take the helm. But his head was fastened to his pillow as with an iron bolt. He grew worse and worse. He must wrestle for his life with a malignant fever.

Where was my lady Hoity then? Pained, beyond a doubt, but pained for herself, not for him. She kept at a prudent distance, lamenting the fate which had deprived her of a certain prize; for, good woman, she fancied herself irresistible. Happily, her nature was of the most elastic constitution; she soon recovered from her misplaced attachment, and actually wondered how she *could*, in the name of common sense, have cared one fig for a merchant on the verge of bankruptcy. He was no beauty, certainly; he was addicted to gin and water, too; his conversation was rather coarse, and his manners decidedly inelegant. She could not account for it; all his imperfections were so glaring. It must have been one of those mysterious infatuations, produced by Lapland witches, or some other horrible cause. She determined to frown down a family which had always held a questionable position, and which was now consigned to merited obscurity. Wise Mrs. Hoity.

Amidst all the sickness, loss, and desolation Gabriel moved about merrily. He had never been so happy; there was almost a glow on his white face, and his large eyes were radiant with joy.

Lel never left her father's bedside; neither remonstrance nor entreaty could entice her away. There, through the long, long nights of delirium, she knelt, calm and tearless, watching every motion, noting every wild word muttered by the invalid. The most practised nurse could not have attended him so tranquilly, so firmly, so judiciously. And when the crisis came, when the sick soul fluttered between life and death, when an hour might make her an orphan, her hand was steady as she bound the ice to his forehead and wiped the water from his face.

"Leave me, Agnes," she would say, "I can do without you." But Agnes, equally inflexible, kept her post. Many and bitter were her tears —bitterer as she thought of the dancing and music which ushered in the blow — the asp in Cleopatra's basket. She looked back upon her former self-confidence as wicked presumption; the hand of God had opened her eyes to her weakness, and in humility and sorrow, deeper than she had ever known, she threw herself in spirit at the foot of the cross, putting all her trust in Him who died there.

There was something of more than mortal splendor in Gabriel's sweet smile as he moved about from Agnes to Lel, from Lel to her father.

The physician was standing doubtfully over the fallen merchant, his finger on the thrilling pulse, his eye on his watch.

"Is there danger?" asked Lel, firmly. "Tell me the truth." The man hesitated.

"As you value a human soul, tell me the truth," she repeated, in a voice stern with emotion.

"There is," was the faint reply. "But the case is far from being desperate."

"Agnes," continued Lel, as firmly as before, though a tremor passed over her, "send for whom you wish."

At a sign from Agnes Gabriel darted like an arrow through the door, followed by the physician. Agnes fell on her knees, praying that, at least an interval of consciousness might be granted. The priest was not long in answering the sick call.

"He is delirious," he said; "we must wait awhile; there is no immediate danger. You should have sent for me sooner; death is a pretty serious matter."

Lel reproached herself for not having yielded to Agnes in the beginning; she thought it might irritate and terrify her father. Now, her only hope was in that diminutive old man, with short gray hair and small gray eyes. Oh, for a moment's reason!

"Pray for him! Pray for him!" said Lel to the priest, seizing his hand. They all knelt together.

Had their united prayer been heard? Was there not a change for the better? Had the body triumphed by its own force?

Two days went by — two days of uncertainty and anguish. Lel left him not a moment. Firm, collected, unrepining, she seemed endowed with supernatural strength. But when her father. once more recognized her, when he called her by name, when he answered her kiss, when he placed his shrunken fingers on her head and blessed her, when the physician pronounced him out of danger, then, indeed, she gave way, fainting in her cousin's arms; then the overtasked body drooped and languished, then her subdued spirit quailed, then came forth the torrent of tears from her bursting heart.

It was a Sunday morning. Agnes was at mass. Melville found the merchant asleep. Lel, too, had fallen asleep on the lounge at the foot of the bed. Then could be seen the ravages which grief and watching had made. Her golden hair no longer met a bloom equal to its own on her cheek; her eyes were hollow, her lips almost bloodless. But amid the wreck was a loveliness infinitely more touching than the glow of health and vigor — the loveliness which, like the flowers "on dreamland graves," only spring from tears. It was "the little more of Agnes" that he had sighed for.

In spite of himself his eyes filled with tears. Lel, the weak mourner, was something precious and holy to him; with all his faults, he was one of the princely few to whom the loved are doubly endeared by poverty and affliction.

He knelt at her feet, a half smile was on her face; he prayed that she might awake, forgive him all the past and promise him all the future. How infinitely nobler is she now than when she sparkled pre-eminent on the crown of fashion. "And over this pure spring," he prayed, "let me be the tree that, taught by her to bloom, may shade and shelter her forever with its arms."

CHAPTER XXI.

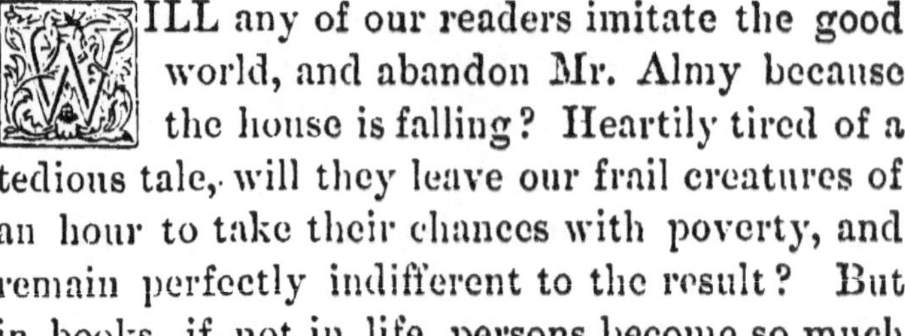

ILL any of our readers imitate the good world, and abandon Mr. Almy because the house is falling? Heartily tired of a tedious tale, will they leave our frail creatures of an hour to take their chances with poverty, and remain perfectly indifferent to the result? But in books, if not in life, persons become so much more attractive in adversity — all our affections are enlisted, we wish we had it in our power to assist them, we would do anything in the wide world — die for them, if necessary; for our sympathy costs us nothing beyond a tear, soon shed and sooner dried.

Agnes had written to her mother for permission to stay and nurse Mr. Almy and comfort Lel. We need not say that this permission was granted, nay, enjoined. The mother's heart was yearning for her daughter, and full of tender fears for her safety; but she wrote: —

"Stay, my child, and do your duty."

Hers was the meek heroism of a self-denying heart, the heroism of which earth is silent and heaven musical. Agnes saw with real pleasure Melville's returning love for Lel; she saw with a smile his complete indifference to herself. She had wounded his pride deeply and bitterly; and wounded pride must revenge itself in some way, though it be in forgiveness. Melville, of course, felt no resentment; but he could not help thinking that Agnes had been too dictatorial; that, in short, she wanted that feminine gentleness which Lel possessed in such an eminent degree. She had spoken to him like a pedantic school-girl, whose mouth was full of set phrases; who firmly believed her wise stereotype sentences an answer to every argument, — revolting cannon adapted to repel, no matter what or where, the attack. He was tempted to laugh at the patronizing air with which she had referred him to Kempis on Nature and Grace; it *could* not have been in humility. And then the parrot-like repetition of — "*By the practice of my religion, — by the practice of my religion,*" as if a person could be any wiser by a participation in the sacraments; as if God would give us light to know our vocation when we employ all the means He has appointed to obtain His grace and direction; as if a young heart could gather wisdom and experience from constant self-examination and the confessional. But worse than this, Agnes had been the cause of pain to Lel; he could not forgive this. She had been the cause of his own fickleness; he could not forgive this either.

If any are disposed — and there must be many — to frown Melville down as an insignificant fellow in spite of his generosity, we pray them to examine well their own hearts before they pronounce sentence. There is a time when we *think* we love, and a time when we *do* love. Melville only *thought* he loved Lel, for she was so gifted, so beautiful, that it was impossible to resist her fascination ; but her levity and wilfulness kept him from being really in love. Is he to be despised for this? Millions have the recklessness, nobleness, selfishness, folly, call it what you will, to sacrifice wisdom for love ; but not one in ten thousand can reverse the case. But there's very little love alive, and less that's worth mentioning. It was only when Lel displayed that might of firmness and affection around her father's bedside ; it was only when she was an outcast from fashion and fortune, when her cheek was pale and wasted, when she needed assistance and comfort, when others were deserting her, when the house was falling ; it was only then, that Melville began to love. Let him be honored for it ; such things are rare.

Mr. Almy was recovering very slowly ; his constitution had been almost fatally shattered ; the physician hoped to restore him by summer. He was well enough, however, to look into the affairs of his house and to resume operations as well as could be done from his pillow. And it must be said that his brother merchants, with scarce an exception, were ready to extend a helping hand. There is a touch of professional pride in almost every department of life, which, though not a Christian virtue, is still a manly laurel, whose leaves adorn the desert through which we journey.

How changed was Lel! A deeper change had taken place than Melville dreamed of, a change produced by suffering and Agnes. On the fly-leaf in her cousin's prayer-book Lel had written in pencil these unpretending lines, which express more than we could do in as many pages:

Who shall comfort, who shall cheer me
  Who shall bid my sorrows cease ?
Is there not a spirit near me,
  Pointing to a land of peace ?
When the tender heart is shaken
  By the hands that blessed before,
When by all the world forsaken,
  Is there nothing, nothing more ?

Who will shelter, who will love me,
  Who will dry the lonely tear ?
Is there not a voice above me,
  Sweetly whispering, " I am near !

> I will ever watch beside thee,
> I will be thy faithful friend;
> Love me, and my love shall guide thee;
> Kneel, and let thy sorrows end !"

Lel had music of her own for this; a simple, mournful melody, such as pious peasants dream of. She was humming it over one evening at at the close of spring in her father's chamber. Mr. Almy was still unable to leave his room; he was sitting in an easy-chair, near the open window that overlooked his garden, and he could once more see the blessed sun and feel the light south winds; he could once more look out upon the green grass and gay flowers below. Agnes had gone to visit some poor people; the father and daughter were alone.

"Come closer to me, Lel," said Mr. Almy; "I will tell you a story." He took her hand in his. "You scarcely remember your mother; I have rarely spoken to you of her. Perhaps you thought I had forgotten her; but no, no, I remembered her too well for my own peace. She was the sweetest and best of human beings; I love Agnes because she reminds me of her."

The fallen merchant paused and pressed his daughter's hand more closely.

"She was a pious, practical Catholic; she never missed mass, not even on the cold winter mornings, when she had to go shivering through the streets before sunrise, whilst I clung to the warm blankets, pitying my good wife's fanaticism.

"When her last lingering illness came she bore it without a murmur. I wish all the philosophers in the universe had seen the meek, patient, joyous fortitude of that Christian woman. I had been an infidel; at least I took pride in passing for one, but my faith in atheism was shaken by the spectacle; for I saw that visible support which humility obtains from heaven; I saw that the God in whom she trusted did not fail her.

"She called me to her deathbed; she placed your hand in mine, as I hold it now, and charged me, with her last breath, to bring you up a Catholic!"

The merchant shuddered; he seemed not to see Lel, she was kneeling with her head on his lap, bathing his hands with her tears.

"*I made the promise, Lel,* I made the promise, and, O God, how have I kept it! When I remember that solemn moment, the smile she gave, when on my knees I made the pledge she asked, that smile which was still on her face when they buried her, it seems like a frightful **dream**, that I could have broken my word, because I was sneered at, because I wished you to enjoy all the standard follies which Catholicity forbids, because I had doomed you in my heart to be a brilliant woman of the world! Am I not a villain? Go home with Agnes, and forget the coward traitor to his wife and his conscience, whom you have loved and honored as a kind, good parent."

In a paroxysm of tears she sprang to his breast, and threw her arms around his neck.

"And I thought I was making some amends by staying at home with you, by inventing amusements to make you happy, by indulging you to excess, and accomplishing your mind and person! Can you forgive me? Can you forgive me, my own dear, injured, martyred child?"

She pressed his head to her bosom, she gave him a long look of unutterable love.

What are all the vows, the sighs, the caresses of chronicled lovers to that holy kiss coming in mercy and love from a daughter's lips?

"Hear me out," he resumed. "I studied Catholicity to justify myself by detecting its errors, and I found its truth. I feared to own it, even to myself; I feared to confess it to the world; the confession would have injured my business, would have made me ridiculous; and so I risked my salvation and yours for that bubble, human esteem, and sought to drown my conscience by nightly potations."

"Thank God, you did not succeed!" cried Lel, embracing him again and again.

"I *did not* succeed," said Mr. Almy. "If ever a man toiled for a false conscience I did; but I did not get it because an angel in heaven was praying for both of us!"

Until then the fallen merchant had not shed a tear; but they came, at last, blissful, blessed drops, that washed away the agony and shame of years. And amid them, though his face was white and haggard, though his eyes were sunken, though the lines on his high forehead were deeper, Lel saw *the expression he ought to have* — the very look she had dreamed of and prayed for.

He folded her to his heart, he dried his tears on her hair, and said, in a voice broken with emotion : —

"*We will meet your mother in heaven!*"

Agnes, who had just entered the room, seeing their agitation, was about to retire, when Mr. Almy called her back.

"You are one of us, Agnes," he said. "Lel will tell you all that has passed between us. There *was* a time," he continued, smiling, "when I was foolish enough to think that you might be one of us in name as well as in spirit. But you have chosen the better part. How tired you must be of helping to nurse me, of gratifying all my whims, of hearing all my complaints, of seeing all my misery. It is a shame for us to keep you here — we can do without you now — at least we have no right to expect you to remain, merely because we would miss you so much."

"I scarcely expected," replied Agnes, "to be dismissed so unceremoniously; but I am determined not to go back to Loretto until your daughter goes with me; and abuse me as you please, I will not stir a step before she is ready."

"It is hard," pursued Mr. Almy, "to keep from hating you, you make such large demands on my gratitude. As for Melville, I shall certainly hate him, unless I become able to repay his magnanimous kindness. It is just like him: there never was a knight in all chivalry equal to him. I do believe he has given me every dollar he has, and is selling his pictures and trinkets to maintain himself from day to day. My house and furniture will bring something; and if I could get amongst my clerks once more I might make a living yet, and do something for Lel."

"Never mind your clerks or me either," said

Lel; "make up your mind to go to Loretto with Agnes as soon as you are able to move about. I will stay here and teach music"——

"Under Mrs. Hoity's protection?" interposed her father.

"Under God's protection?" cried Lel; "and with these little fingers will build you a cottage near the convent, where we may spend the rest of our lives together."

"Will those little fingers pay off Melville, too?" said her father.

"One finger of her right hand alone would more than pay him," answered Agnes.

A blush passed over Lel's face, succeeded by the most painful thought. There was a struggle going on in that young heart, to which few so young, so impulsive, so capable of love are equal. Melville had too much delicacy to declare himself so soon after a refusal from Agnes; the misfortunes of her father, and her own altered position, in which a lover, equally generous, but less refined, would have seen an excuse for precipitation, only served to deter him from a step which might seem forced by compassion, or taken in the hope that if *he* had been fickle, *she* was poor and desolate enough now to forgive and gratefully welcome him back.

"Was Gabriel with you?" said Mr. Almy to Agnes, breaking the awkward pause.

"I have not seen him since morning," she replied.

We must here remark a change in Mr. Almy towards Gabriel. Formerly the proud merchant regarded him with ill-concealed aversion; he seemed to think him an impertinent intruder, an officious busybody, always blundering and always out of place. Whenever he spoke to him it was with a scowl, full of hatred, yet not unmingled with fear. But as soon as the fever left him it was different; he loved to have Gabriel near him; he welcomed his pale face to his bedside, and was never happier than when Gabriel would come and sit by him and smile him to sleep. Perhaps the young man's kindness had won his heart, perhaps adversity had taught him forgiveness, perhaps there was another reason. Be this as it may, Mr. Almy and Gabriel were friends. This meek, benevolent creature had never resented the merchant's insults; at times he would disappear for weeks and then return as humble, as charitable, as uncomplaining as ever. No wonder, then, he replied to advances so warmly made; he scarcely knew the meaning of revenge, and no one ever appealed to him in affliction without finding a friend.

It is the bright month of June ; Mr. Almy is nearly well. Again that good priest, that diminutive old man, with short gray hair and small gray eyes, is in the house. He had been there more than once ; he had brought books there ; he had been alone with Mr. Almy hours at a time.

It is a Sunday morning in July ; the bells are ringing for early mass—it is the feast of St. Vincent of Paul. The good priest is at the altar, and, at the communion railing, Agnes, Gabriel, Lel, and Mr. Almy are kneeling side by side.

There are two more stanzas pencilled in the prayer-book : —

> I have sought thee, I have found thee
>   Lamb of mercy, holy guest;
> Thy eternal love has bound thee
>   Captive in a mortal breast.
> Oh, that I had sooner tasted
>   Joys I never knew before!
> Oh, had I the youth I wasted,
>   Back again, to live it o'er!—
>
> Oh, that I had sooner known thee,
>   Oh, could I the past recall
> Yet thou wilt not now disown me
>   Father of the Prodigal!

To my breast, thy Son, descending,
Sweetly there appeals for me;
Let me then, thus humbly bending,
Pledge the rest of life to thee!—

Mr. Almy's conversion was by no means great an event as his failure.

"It is very natural," observed Mrs. Hoity, "that a falling family should choose an unfashionable religion. And as for Lel," she said, "she would turn Turk or anything else to please her father." And these wise remarks embodied the opinion of the world in general. In a few days, however, the world ceased to have an opinion; and Mr. Almy was permitted to go to his counting-room without being cross-questioned or stared at.

The dwelling-house and furniture were advertised for public sale; Lel and Agnes were preparing to revisit Loretto.

Melville determined to speak; it was Lel's last day in town; he could not part from her without an explanation; she was so frail, so spirit-like, he might never see her again.

The moment came; his elaborate excuses, his long professions all failed him. He knelt to the injured girl, and uttered the single words, "I love you."

Lel was calm and smiling; the struggle had

taken place, the victory was gained before she went to communion.

"You tell me that you love me," said Lel ; "it may be, and my weak heart is willing to believe it. I thought so once before ; you know how much I was mistaken. I need not say that the gift of your fortune 'to my impoverished father has not diminished my regard. If I do not admit that I love you, I confess that I shall never love another. But I cannot accept your addresses for a year, *and not then* "—her voice faltered — "*unless you are a Catholic!*"

While the words were ringing in his ears she hurried from the room and threw herself into Agnes' arms. Lel ! Lel ! thou tender girl, there is not a hero in history with a soul like thine. Yet the world has cast thee off ; it has forgotten thee—even *he*, the first and last choice of thy heart, may forget thee too, for thou hast renounced him. But weep not, weep not, Lel ; the angels are around thee, and all the saints of heaven are smiling, as thy heavenly Father accepts and records the sacrifice thou hast made!

And that night Lel had a dream —the same she had at Loretto. She dreamed that she was in the convent chapel, alone, at midnight ; that as she was kneeling there a lady, whose face was concealed by a white veil spangled with stars, ap-

peared upon the altar.   Slowly and noiselessly
the figure moved towards her and stood over her
— the veil was uplifted — is was her mother!
Not the pale, cold body she had seen in the coffin,
but the mild, warm, bright being, whose breast
had once been her home — the living mother of
other days.   Still more radiant was her smile
when she stooped and kissed her, saying, " *Now
you are mine!* "

There is another figure on the altar — another
Mother, but infinitely more beautiful, infinitely
more tender ; and from her hands and forehead
are streaming rays of glory that bathe the sanctuary in light.   And as she stood, a child appeared upon her breast, whose lustre eclipsed her
own ; a halo trembled around his head, and he
stretched forth his little hands to the sleeper, and
she awoke with a prayer on her lips and her
heart full of joy and hope.

The morning was just beginning to break ;
Agnes was kneeling over her friend, her face
wet with tears.

"What," said Lel, glancing at her cousin's
undisturbed bed, " have you been up all night ?"

"I have been thinking of my past presumption," replied Agnes ; " it is enough to keep me
awake.   In the pride of my heart I came here
thinking that I was an angel commissioned to

save and instruct you; I regarded you with a sort of compassion, lamenting that you had not the heart to love God as I did. Oh, Lel, our Father in heaven has vouchsafed me a glance into my own heart, and I tremble at the knowledge of what evil I am capable. Had my education been like yours I should be a victim and a scourge. Even now, I might not relinquish human love, as you are doing. You have been dreaming sweetly; let me kiss this pure temple, in which God is dwelling."

"My own Agnes," said Lel, returning her embrace, "I owe all that I am to your example, and so does my father. Had my mother lived, I might have escaped many a sin, but I never should have been what you are. Dear, dear Agnes, you have more to contend with in one hour than I in a lifetime."

The sun had risen, and the two friends went forth to communion. Never had Lel felt such a transport of joy and peace; and if Agnes was pale with watching, her face was calmer and nobler than it had ever been. These are the morning walks that give health and bliss, that lead to a country of perpetual green and unfading flowers, where the spirit never sickens or languishes, where all is freshness, light, and music.

The carriage was at the door to perform its last family service; it was to be sold that morning. Mr. Almy silently folded Agnes and Lel to his breast, mutely blessed them, and walked away, leaving them in charge of Melville. The old black coachman drew his rough sleeve across his eyes and drove off. Lel watched the old house, the old house where she was born, where her mother died, where she had first wept and smiled, where she had learned to love her father, where she had frolicked as a child, romped as a girl, danced as a woman; the old house where she had first met Melville, and lost and regained him; where little Clarence had dined and wondered; where so many a match was made, so many a vow spoken and broken; where her little fingers had first trickled as aimlessly as rain-drops over the piano; the old house immortal with Beethoven's Sonatas and Mendelssohn's trios; where Handel, Haydn, Mozart, Weber, Meyerbeer, Heller, Thalberg, Schuberth, Schulhoff, Listz, clustered like familiar genii around Aladdin's lamp, awaiting the touch of its mis-tress; the old house endeared by so many years of joy, consecrated by so many months of pain; where she had nursed her father, where she had heard his story, where they had taken together the first blessed draught at the well-spring of

Catholicity, where they had breakfasted after communion, where she had dreamed of her two mothers and the divine babe on the altar. She watched it with a swelling heart as long as it was in sight, for she loved it as if it lived.

Gabriel met them at the cars.

"Do not leave my father," said Lel.

"He does not need me now," whispered Gabriel. "I serve another master," he added, looking at Melville.

Before leaving the carriage Lel had taken a silver medal from her wrist and thrown it over Melville's neck.

"Wear it," she said, "and say the prayer whenever you think of me. I shall be happy if I serve to remind you of heaven."

The cars are gliding off. Farewell!

At ten o'clock Melville wandered up to Mr. Almy's; a red flag is waving from Lel's window. He shuddered, his knees shook, the dreary, blank existence before him was worse than death. But he had a duty to perform; sad as it was, there was hope and consolation in it. Lel he had not, but no other had her, and no other should have her piano.

CHAPTER XXII.

 SAY, Charley," chuckled the Colonel, "These are fine birds, fine birds. I don't think I missed a single shot."

The old gentleman had spent the afternoon woodchuck shooting, and his bag was handsomely filled. Though a poor angler, as we have seen, he was a capital shot; in fact, he shot well enough to be called Colonel without any other pretension to the title.

He was returning home, a little fatigued, but flushed with success, and longing for some good friends to partake of the supper he promised himself that very night, when he saw a carriage passing along the road towards Loretto. He could see it plainly although hidden from it by the woods. All at once the dogs, who were ranging ahead, set up a bark and scampered after the carriage. Neither Charley nor the Colonel could whistle them back. Away they went, like those faithful hounds in Burger's ballad.

"That's strange," muttered the Colonel.

"I'll bet it's Miss Agnes!" shouted Charley.

Taking fire at the suggestion, the Colonel bounded forward and cleared the fence as though a bullet had never made a hole in his leg. Agnes ought to have written word the very day 'she meant to arrive instead of leaving it uncertain.

' And now, my dear reader, you are again at Loretto. The forest trees are in leaf, the orchards heavy with fruit, the spring flowers have passed away, and the busy bees have exhausted the honeysuckles wreathing the white porches. Agnes is in her mother's arms, and all those anxious moments, all those trembling fears, all those sleepless nights and weary days are forgotten as the tearful widow strains to her heart her only child. What matters it that she is thinner and paler, that there is no longer a particle of the girl in her face, that she is no longer young? she had her back again, safe and sound, and in the joy of the moment she asked no more.

Lel, too, was in her arms — no longer the thoughtless, merry girl; no longer buoyant with life, health, and hope, darting here and there like a butterfly; no longer the flattering tease, the spoiled favorite of fashion; but Lel the mourner, Lel the Catholic. Yet, to the mother's eye, Agnes had changed most; for Lel was happy in her faith, and her joyous soul, though rudely shaken, was still ready to leap up again, as the young tree resumes its place when the storm that bent it is over. It was not so with Agnes. Why?

"*When I left yóu*," she said to her mother that night, "*I felt sure of heaven; now I do not.*"

The Colonel embraced Lel and Agnes, and Agnes and Lel. He could not tell, for the life of him, which he loved most. They had come just in time for his woodcock; and Charley, with the big drops of delight dancing in his eyes, put forth all his skill on the precious birds.

After tea they took a walk down the road — Agnes with her mother, Lel with the Colonel. Lel had never seen Loretto in summer; the hand of a fairy seemed to have passed over the place; all round her was beauty and repose. The lark was gliding lazily to bed; the night-hawk was wheeling and darting through the air; the cows were soberly walking home "as if conscious of human affection;" the sheep were lying down in white groups for the night; the trees sighed in the evening wind; and the distant spire of the convent was colored by the crimson clouds on which the sun was still shining from beneath the horizon. There was a holy calm in Lel's breast, as beautiful and profound as the repose of the scene on which she gazed.

"Why did not Almy come?" exclaimed the Colonel. "We would have made him a boy again."

" Why *could* he not?" thought Lel; but she was silent.

And when the stars stole out, when the whip-poor-will was heard in the woods, when the frogs began their nightly serenade to their parent stream, our four friends betook themselves to the porch.

" Why didn't you bring Melville with you," said the Colonel, darting his cigar at a perse-vering gnat, " or some other young gentleman, instead of returning like two old maids ? "

" As we are," added Lel.

" Nonsense ! " simpered the Colonel, confound-ing his little persecutor with a prodigious puff. " What do you think of the world, Agnes ? rather a nice place after all, eh ? Oh, I have had my time in it ! "

" And so have I," said Agnes.

" You ought to see more of it, my girl."

" No, thank you, I have seen quite enough."

" Why, you jade, you, what have you seen in a month ? It takes one years to see the world as it is in all its majestically accumulating glory and versatile interest. Poh ! " continued the Colonel, " what have *you* seen ? "

" I have seen," returned Agnes, with provok-ing calmness, " that its standard of morality is not God's standard ; that wealth and imprudence are its virtues; poverty and modesty its vices; that money is its god, its grand governing principle, to which all else is subservient; that happiness is measured by the purse, and that a comfortable if not luxurious settlement in life is the grand goal, in the chase of which eternity is lost sight of."

"Poh!" ejaculated the Colonel.

"I have seen Catholics almost universally ashamed of the first principles of their faith, and artfully smoothing them over to attract their dissenting brethren. I have seen them dressing so indecently, even when priests are invited, that their pastors are put to the blush."

"That's the priests' fault," mumbled the Colonel.

"I have seen," continued Agnes, smiling at the interruption, "that your happy, merry men and women are only so because they have a false conscience which has ceased to accuse them; I have seen all who have virtue enough to feel living in perpetual fear of the temptations by which they are surrounded. I have seen that society is but a hollow farce, in which there is neither love nor friendship. I have seen the idol of a thousand worshippers left without a single friend when touched by poverty."

The Colonel groaned and looked away from Lel.

"And I have seen," said Agnes, taking her uncle's hand and modulating her voice to a whisper, "I have seen, that in spite of all this, the world is dazzlingly beautiful, winning, enchanting. And oh, my dear, good uncle, it is not *God* that makes it so! I have felt its insidious fascination. I tell you, uncle, that I have been wandering along the brink of a precipice; that I could no more live in the world than can the moth live in the candle; that my only salvation is in that convent!"

The old man knocked the ashes carefully from his cigar, slowly brushed a tear from his eye, and put his arm around Lel's neck.

"Thank God, *you* are not a Catholic!" he exclaimed. "There are no Protestant convents to take *you* from me."

With tears streaming down her cheeks, Lel leaned her head on his shoulder. A horrible suspicion ran through the Colonel's mind. He raised her head in the clear moonlight, and mutely questioned her, with such a fearful, timid gaze, that her heart bled for him as she said:—

"Yes, uncle, I *am* a Catholic!"

The cigar fell from his hand, his cane rolled on the porch, his broad chest swelled as if his heart was bursting; had they both been dead at his feet he could scarcely have shown more grief than at this overthrow of all his plans, this defeat of his best diplomacy.

"Checkmated!" he sobbed, in uncontrolled agony, repulsed them sternly from his side, and then, spreading his arms, snatched them both to his bosom. "Checkmated! Checkmated!"

One word; the sermon just preached by Agnes against the world has nothing new in it; Solomon put it all in a nutshell long ago; it will be found better expressed in every prayer-book. To the Colonel it was perfectly puerile, the same old song which saints and misanthropists have been singing together from time immemorial. Only by constant meditation do we comprehend that life is but a preparation for death; and unless this great truth is realized where is the folly in living as if time were the main thing and eternity a trifle? The visible present, though brief, and bounded by the grave, is apt to be more important than the invisible future. Without strong *faith* men *must* live as they do; and all who reprove them for neglecting their souls, in over-devotion to their bodies, will seem only fools, or very good people who have not weighed well the difficulty of what they propose. Every day we witness the same spectacle, a world, for whom God died upon the cross, devoting all their time, all their thoughts to obtain material comfort and avoid sorrow, a prayer at night, an ejaculation in the morning — the rest of the day sacred to the body. We see this every day; we do not wonder at it, it is all right, all in the order of Providence; the only mystery is, that some weak, pious souls are absurd enough to quit the world and devote the greater part of their lives to religious exercises; this is the singular part of it. It would be an unnatural state of things, indeed, if all mankind were to make business secondary to religion, and spend as much time in praising God as they do in making money.

Why, the best instructed, the most edifying Catholic parents cannot help preferring an auspicious alliance with man for their daughters to an eternal union with God in the solitary cloister; and how can we expect the worldly-minded Colonel, who has not seen a confessional for forty years, to consider the choice made by Agnes as anything else than a burning shame, a living death? How many of us have realized, by prayer and meditation, that heaven is all and earth nothing? How many of us are truly sick of the vanity of life, much as we pretend to be, and do not sagely conclude that our neighbors and ourselves are all doing our duty, taking our share of enjoyment with sufficient gratitude, and bearing our just proportion of affliction with exemplary resignation?

There was a time when monasteries and chapels were as numerous as castles, when the Christian world seemed ambitious to live a Christian life, when self-denial and self-castigation were honored, when the consecration of a Cathedral was of more moment than the opening of a railroad, when there was something nobler than science and dearer than profit, when the security of government was in the humility of the people, when the security of the people was in the firmness and purity of the church, when there was not, as now, a groundwork of ignorance, pride, and envy, which is either a withering master or a dangerous slave. Yes, there was a time when all this was, and when Agnes might not have been laughed at, but it was in the dark ages, reader, in those terrible nights before the sunlight of newspapers had illumined the earth. '

Must it be told that within a month after her return from the city Agnes entered the convent as a candidate; that three months later her long hair was cut to suit the brown cap of the novice? Until her hair was cut the Colonel had cherished a hope that she would repent her girlish haste; but when he saw the ruin caused

by those envious shears he could not help saying,
"It is all over, all over." And ye who have
clung to Agnes in the hope that she would be
induced to marry Melville, or incline to Mr.
Almy, or that some romantic young gentleman
would appear upon the carpet, invested with
every virtue and every grace, between whom
and our young novice a sweet sympathy might
be established which should ultimately lead to
better things than the cloister, and supply a
chapter or two of delicious sentiment, leave us,
we beseech you, for her CHOICE is made, though
the vows are not yet taken. Yes, she is lost
to the world, that sweet, beautiful girl, who
laughed so merrily with her load of premiums
in her arms; the milk-white lamb amongst those
green hills; the friend who had gone to change
Lel, and who did change her, though she nearly
perished in the effort; the kind protectress who
had comforted little Clarence and the Wanderer;
the keen-sighted woman' who had penetrated
the secret of Mr. Almy's face, who had conquered Melville and reigned supreme in the
ball-room, eclipsing all the practised belles of
the season. *She was lost to the world*, that
sweet, beautiful girl, who was so well fitted to
delight and adorn it, lost before the first bloom
of youth had passed from her cheeks, before

experience had dried the first bright waters of hope and trust that are born in our hearts ; lost before there was any need to seek a refuge from the ills of life in that last resource, a convent. *She is lost to the world*, and what matters it what *she* has gained, what heaven has won. So thought the Colonel.

Yet what was his love for Agnes compared to her mother's, the mother who remembered her baptism, her first cries, her first words, her first caresses; who had counted her first smiles and treasured them in her heart; who remembered every incident of her youth, her first lisping prayers, her first songs, her first visit to mass, her first confession, her first communion, her confirmation. What was his bereavement to *hers?* Agnes was her only child, her only companion in prayer, her jewel, her treasure, her all on earth; a thousand uncles could not have loved her as she did; their lives had been one, and now they are called upon to live apart. Oh, not *apart!* Who shall say apart? When they are repeating, day after day and night after night, the same dear litanies, when they are appealing to the same saints, the same angels, the same Blessed Mother, the same Father, Son and Holy Ghost, when they are living together in God, who shall say they are living apart?

And thus thought Mrs. Cleveland, and she missed not her daughter's long, dark hair; and if she shed floods of natural tears it was not because her daughter was clad in the plain livery of heaven. And so thought Lel, and she was glad of the CHOICE, though she had now to sit and sew alone, though she had to walk alone, though she had to watch the sun rise and set, and play Beethoven, and listen to the birds and pluck wild flowers and muse under the old oak-trees without Agnes at her side.

CHAPTER XXIII.

WHO shall say what passed in Agnes' heart after that memorable Thursday evening? What visions of worldly happiness crowded on her soul, outshining and eclipsing the silent convent to which she had pledged herself? Before her first visit to the city she had wondered how others could be so thoughtless as to abandon themselves to the insignificant pleasures which she despised, and which had not brilliancy enough even to tempt her. But on a sudden her soul had risen up in arms against her. The triumphs and the joys which had been contemptible now danced before her eyes in fearful fascination. They beckoned her on through a lovely vista, opening into sunshine and soft splendor, where roses were blooming, where trees were bending over glittering fountains, dropping luscious, golden fruit. She had measured herself with those who had sneered at the country girl; she had overtopped them and moved amongst them like a queen. She had perceived her superiority — it had been tacitly admitted — she saw a brilliant career before her, she had only to step forward and enjoy it.

Was this not a temptation? We have written to no purpose if Agnes is still considered a cold, calm, passionless creature. We have written to no purpose if the likeness to her father has not been detected by more than Lel. Few minds could spin such glancing, silky webs for the winged soul; few hearts could feel the enchantment of fancy so deeply. Yet how little did she know this, when she knelt for her confessor's permission to save Lel, feeling certain of her own salvation!

She recalled the haughtiness with which she had referred Melville to Kempis on Nature and Grace, as if she were perfect in that sublime chapter. Oh, Agnes, Agnes, was there not pride, presumption, in thy self-confidence? was there not too much contempt for others, whom thou didst believe weaker than thyself? She admitted it in tears before the cross.

And the world, the world which thou hast scorned, is it not rather to be feared than dared? is it not rather to be pitied and prayed for than spurned and denounced? Didst thou not exempt thyself from the censure which thou didst pass on that same world, and think thyself better than the rest of mankind? Ay, even during the conversation with the Colonel on the porch, when the moon was shining, the evening of thy return, didst thou apply to thyself the condemnation so liberally bestowed on thy neighbors?

What would she not have given for that perfect repose, that calm delight she felt before leaving Loretto! Would it never return? Yet why so covetous of spiritual enjoyment, so restless under that spiritual desolation with which the saints themselves are visited? But in the tumult of leaving her mother — and such a mother! — there could not be that fulness of joy to which she had looked forward so eagerly. Not until the moment of parting did Agnes know how much was due that meek, uncomplaining guardian of her youth. How imperfectly had she returned that mother's tender love, how often had she been wanting in affection, how little had she done to console, to amuse, to reward her for those early lessons of piety without which her life might have been a warning!

Oh no! it was not on entering the convent that the young candidate's soul was at rest. A week's retreat! She had proved her own nothingness; she had discovered that all her strength came from God; that, without humility, she was powerless; that the finger of heaven had pointed out her vocation, not as an honor due her virtue, but as a mercy granted to her weakness. She looked up with reverence and love to the old sisters around her, who were preparing to die as they had lived, and begged them to pray that, like them, she might persevere to the close. But that perfect repose, that calm delight, would not return! That spiritual desolation would not pass away! As the traveller in the desert pants for the palm-tree's shade and running waters, as the weary schoolboy sighs for a Christmas holiday, as the wanderer longs for the sweet home he left behind him, so Agnes had sighed and longed for the beginning of her religious life, as if every aspiration would then be instantaneously gratified, as if the unspeakable rapture of that moment would exceed all the transports of youth and innocence. But instead of this it is a time of tears and trial, a time of doubt and fear, in which not one of these bright promises was fulfilled. Oh, could she fling herself once more on her mother's breast and die! Is heaven so hard to win? Is it not easy to be a Sister of Charity? Courage, thou noble girl!

The fervor that carried thee so joyously to communion when thou wast a girl; the devotion that led thee to the city to save thy young cousin, this is something, but something more must thou have to be a Sister of Charity. Let the long hours of meditation pass heavily; let thy thoughts wander painfully to thy dear mother; let thy bosom ache even in the chapel; let thy pillow be steeped in nightly tears; a day of consolation may come, when the sand in the hourglass shall glide away unnoticed; when thy Blessed Mother in heaven shall absorb thy thoughts; when thy breast shall swell with joy before the altar; when thy pillow shall have no thorn.

Whilst Agnes was thus advancing in the school of the cross, Lel undertook to accomplish herself in all the departments of country life. She rose before the sun, and (gentle reader, wince not!) fed the chickens, pigeons, geese, ducks, and turkeys; she learned that corn was planted and wheat sown; she was initiated into the mysteries of milking, creaming, churning, curds, and cheese; and her rural ambition endeared her to every hand about the place, to the dairymaid in particular. She knew the names of all the birds, and could distinguish them by their notes; the lark, the plover, the robin, the quail, the woodcock, the flicker, the blackbird, were no longer strangers, but familiar friends. She loved to take the shade with the reapers at nooning, and laugh and jest with them; and there, with her green sun-bonnet cast carelessly aside, and her back against the rough tree, few would have recognized in our Lel the admitted leader of fashion, the reigning star of many a winter.

Her daily rides, her daily rambles over the fields in search of new flowers, had embrowned her clear cheeks and forehead; and, cheered and reinvigorated by exercise and these innocent pastimes, the lightness, fulness, freshness of health returned, and her step was once more as free as air, and her figure rounded to its former symmetry.

But if she loved to stray over the farm with the Colonel and listen to his piscatorial exploits, still more did she love to accompany Mrs. Cleveland through the neighborhood, until she knew the road to every cottage that needed charity. And the people testified their gratitude by saying *she was another Agnes:* they knew no higher compliment. There was another pleasure; once a week, not oftener, she went with her aunt and uncle to see Agnes, and the two friends would visit that dear old confessor who had made the name of Ellen Almy a household word in the convent. And Lel wrote so many sweet, simple hymns, and was so good and kind, that the sisters loved her too, and their prayers were still offered up for her peace and happiness.

And, twice a week she received letters from her father — long letters, letters that she might read and read again, and then file away in her little desk as so many treasures. He was well and doing well. He promised to come soon and spend a fortnight with her. Was she not happy? Did she never languish for that brilliant circle which was still moving without her, and sigh for her place there? Never — never. If, at times, a fear would cross her mind, that the world might regain its fatal hold on her father his next letter drove the thought away. True, she longed to be with him; she begged him to let her return and stay at his side, no matter where he was, or what might happen;

that her health was restored; that she would be ·
happier with him. But˙he forbade it, and she
submitted. It was better to be away from Melville, and she tried not to think of him, save
when she prayed for that generous friend.

Mrs. Cleveland could ill have spared this kind
and loving girl; the Colonel could not have
existed without her. The loss of Agnes did not
grieve him long, for, with the· facility of old
age, he transferred his love to Lel, and thought
that Agnes had never taken half the interest in
his tackle, guns, and hounds that Lel did; and
Charley, unconsciously following in his master's
wake, boldly pronounced — out of his mistress'
hearing, however — that Miss Lel was worth
two of Miss Agnes. Most of our readers will
side with Charley.

CHAPTER XXIV.

ANY one who has derived his chief
pleasure from the society of one family,
instead of relying on himself or on the
everlasting many, and has been suddenly deprived of this sole dependence, will sympathize
with Melville. For years he had seen Lel,

almost daily, but he knew not, until they parted, that she was more than half his existence. He could easily understand why Lel should reject his addresses for a year, for he had given her reason to suspect his constancy ; but not to hear him then unless he was a Catholic amazed and confounded him. He knew that the Catholic Church discouraged mixed marriages, and he would not have been surprised at such a declaration from an Italian peasant girl, but such bigotry in the high-bred, accomplished, and beautiful Lel was a mystery. Had she fallen a victim to those Jesuitical doctrines by which the noblest minds in the world have been perverted? Had she stifled the sweet voice of nature in her soul at the bidding of a black-gowned priest of Rome? It must be so! There is an insuperable barrier between them! Lel was in earnest ; he could trust her word as an infant trusts its mother's smile. There was no change in her love, and the knowledge of this was another pang, for he *never could* be a Catholic. It was out of the question — absurd — impossible.

He had her piano — there was some comfort in that — and would sit for hours brooding over the finger-board, strumming fragments of Lel's favorite pieces ; but the instrument was dead ; the animating spirit was gone, gone forever! In the evenings he was reasonably happy in Mr. Almy's society — they lodged together — but the long, cheerless days were almost insupportable. Feeling the necessity of employment, to save himself from constant despondency, he resumed, with a view to practice, the study of medicine, in which he had already taken a diploma; not that he wanted money, for Mr. Almy had partially repaid him with half the sales of the house and furniture. His generosity to the Almys was known — Mr. Almy had taken no pains to conceal it — but this was not much to his credit with the world. The world is never well pleased when called on to admire virtues it does not practise. Indeed, Melville was looked upon as a tender-hearted, credulous mortal, who had been duped out of a large fortune by the wiles of an old merchant and the blandishments of an artful young girl. They respected him, however for being prudent enough not to marry Lel, and detected in this wise resolve a glimmering of good sense amidst his folly. So powerfully had his insane behavior operated on society that his former intimates were disposed to cut his acquaintance, and it was only when they heard *he still had something left* that their disgust melted into patronizing pity.

Under these auspices Melville might hope to

start in his new profession with tolerable success. His manners were pleasing; his attainments considerable; and, with proper patronage, he was still a desirable match. If the silly fellow would only give up the Almys all might go well with him, and he might even aspire to Mrs. Hoity's occasional notice. This majestic and good-hearted soul never met him without sneering at Lel, until he wished the portly widow a man, that he might dash her to the ground and set his foot on her neck. Once, in speaking of Lel, she said to him with a wink : —

"Poor little creature, how hard she tried to get you ! "

"It is false, madam," cried Melville, "I tried all I could to get *her*, and failed ! I would give more for one hair of her head than for your parlor full of the proudest and richest of this city."

This reckless and unpardonable speech sealed Melville's fate. There was no hope in the upper circles after that; his practice must come from the lower classes.

Melville found abundant occupation in his medical books; but occupation is not always consolation. There was a void in his bosom that pathology could not fill. As for Gabriel, he was a poor companion, with his pale face and uneasy whisper. Almy was his main stay — for did not Lel write long letters to her father every week? and did not her father read some passages from rustic life to a very attentive listener?

One evening, to Melville's consternation and regret, Mr. Almy brought home to tea the diminutive old priest with short gray hair and small gray eyes. Melville could scarcely salute him with ordinary civility; he regarded him as the author of all his anguish, the thief who had stolen away his Lel. Mr. Almy had never seen such a bitter cloud on his room-mate's brow; there was something dangerous in it. Our friend, the priest, did not seem to notice it; or, if he did, was not visibly moved by the gathering storm, having probably encountered rougher weather in his lifetime.

"I have been trying," said Mr. Almy, "to make this young gentleman a Catholic, and as my success has not been very flattering I am disposed to hand him over to you. He is a good scholar, and could easily read the fathers of the church."

"Yes," said the old man, "very good reading. But you don't want to be a priest, do you, Mr. Melville?"

"Not exactly, sir," replied Melville, haughtily.

"No," said the other. "Then, I think the little

catechism would be better than the fathers. Do you know anything about us, Mr. Melville?"

"Something," returned Melville, with startling bitterness. "I know that you have rendered me hopelessly miserable, by depriving me of a bless. ing that I might now enjoy, but for the heartless tyranny you exercise over all who are weak enough to admit your power."

"Is that all you know?" asked the priest.

"It is all I wish to know!" thundered Melville, incensed at his antagonist's calmness. "Have you a right to plunge two, who love each other, into an abyss of despair that the predilections of the pope may be gratified? I tell you, sir, that all the bishops in Christendom cannot love as I do that sweet victim of their superstition!"

"You *do* seem to be quite in love," said the priest.

"Had you a right," continued Melville, "to dissuade her from marrying me because I was not in your communion? Have I ever done any thing unbecoming a man or a Christian? Am I not as honest as thousands who seek your confessional?"

"These question's are rather hard to answer," began the other with a smile. "I believe you are a very good man, though you are in a sad passion now. I claim a right to advise in all these cases, and hold myself accountable to God alone. I have been accused of being a match-maker, but this is the first time I have been up-braided as a match-breaker."

"You mean to say, sir," answered Melville, "that you never had so much reason to save a young lady from such a villain as I!"

"I mean to say nothing of the kind. How do I know whether you are a villain or not? All I know is that you are not a Christian, and that Lel is too good for any heathen on the face of the earth."

"She is indeed," muttered Melville, white with rage. "If your persecution were confined to me alone, I could endure it, and console myself with despising you. But are you not well aware that you are exacting a sacrifice from her which must be fatal to her happiness.

The old man smiling in his face, replied:—

"Don't you think she can live without you?" so innocently, that Mr. Almy laughed outright.

Goaded to madness, Melville turned on Mr. Almy, gasping between his teeth, "I little ex-pected to be mocked by *you*."

The significant emphasis of *you* brought a deep blush to Mr. Almy's cheek, and he shaded his eyes with his hand.

"Gentlemen," continued Melville, rising, "if you expect to make a convert of me by practising upon my love you are sadly mistaken. The game you are playing may break my heart, but it shall never make me the hypocritical proselyte of a faith I despise."

So saying he left the room, followed by Gabriel. He went to his bedroom, and, trembling in every limb, threw himself on a chair. An even temper like his, when fully roused, is terrible; his lips were white as death, while his cheeks and forehead burned like fire. Lel would not have known him as he sat there, glaring at the candle with a steady glazed eye.

"They shall find," he said, clenching his hand, "that I am not a lump of mere dough to be moulded according to the whim of a weak-minded girl, or a cold, calculating priest. And then, to be laughed at! By heaven, they shall see that my patience, like my fortune, has an end!"

"He felt a hand laid on his shoulder; it was Gabriel's.

"Have you too come," he shouted, springing to his feet. "Have you followed me here to heap insult on insult, and gloat over the shame of an injured man? Leave me!" and, seizing the youth by the throat, he strove to hurl him against the wall.

Melville was a man of great strength, and the
quivering sinews rose like whip-cords in his arms.
But with all his power, doubled by nervous excitement, and put forth to the utmost, he could
not force that pale youth an inch from his place,
or wrench that white hand from his shoulder.

Gabriel was another being. As a storm
gathers in the sky, which has been tranquil all
the summer, instead of that sweet, unchanging
smile there was a withering frown, before which
the boldest might tremble. Melville quailed
under his indignant eye.

"You make me blush for you," said Gabriel,
turning away from him. "Be calm!"

"Calm!" echoed Melville, with a harsh laugh.
"Did you not see how that hoary old badger
exulted over the wreck of the life which he has
blighted? Did you not hear him call me a villain, and did you not hear that thankless merchant, for whom I have offered up my last cent,
and for whom I would have staked my life —
did you not hear *him* — Mr. Almy; *her* father,
applaud his deliberate malice with a fiendish
laugh?"

"No, said Gabriel, his breast heaving as he
spoke. "But I heard you, without cause or provocation, insult a feeble old man, too wise and
too weak to resent your abuse! I heard you,

without cause or provocation, turn against a friend and upbraid him for receiving a favor which you have cancelled by this untimely and ungenerous boasting. If you have a spark of manliness left you should go down on your knees and beg pardon of that old man, whose heart is full of love for you, and of that friend who would have done as much or more for you without making it a reproach and a theme of self-glorification!"

Melville resumed his seat and leaned his head on the table. As Gabriel watched him the frown vanished, the smile returned. Melville held his hand over his eyes; presently he stretched it out to Gabriel, who pressed it between both of his—it was covered with tears.

"Come closer to me!" said Melville.

The smile on that strange being's face brightened as he advanced, and with feminine tenderness threw his arm around the mourner's neck. Melville caught the pale stripling to his breast, and, as he did so, a load of sorrow seemed to glide from his heart, and he wept like a repentant boy. Happy are those who have a friend in whose arms they can indulge, without fear or shame, the outpouring of a wounded soul, through whom the torrent of grief can pass away, which must else ravage the breast within which it is bound! Then an hour suffices to dismiss the agony which years could not conquer; and afterward the rainbow comes, and the sun of promise breaks forth, and the drops that have fallen turn to verdure and flowers! But one has seen the storm, and all may see the sunshine and wonder how it can be so. Such friends are few, but Gabriel was one of them.

Melville turned from Gabriel to his dear piano, which was consecrated by all the blessed past; he thought that Lel sat there and watched him. He drew her medal from his breast and kissed it; then kneeling for the first time, he remembered his promise, he repeated aloud, —

"Oh Mary, conceived without sin, pray for us who have recourse to thee!"

When he rose he hesitated for an instant — it was but an instant — with his hand on the door, then disappeared.

The old man had risen to go, his hat in one hand, his cane in the other. His small gray eyes began to twinkle as Melville introduced himself, evidently with peaceful purposes.

"I recall all that I have said — I knew not what I was saying," said Melville, pronouncing the words with difficulty. "I have played but a poor part before you, and beg you to forgive me and pray for me."

Those small gray eyes began to twinkle more
and more; perhaps a slight film overspread
them. He put down his hat, then his cane on
top of it, and extending both arms, shook Melville's hands warmly in his.

"My dear friend," he said, "I forgive you and
will continue to pray for you. You have lost a
treasure which I am glad to see you prize, and I
confess that I am in part responsible for the
loss. I am not surprised that you do not rank
me amongst your friends, after an act of duty,
which may well provoke one so uninstructed as
you are in the first principles of our holy faith.
Do come and see me. I will tell you all I know
about the church which Lel has joined. Good-
night"—he took his hat and cane, "Good-night;
God bless you; good-night, Mr. Almy." And so
this simple, pious man took leave of our two
friends.

They sat together in silence, which Melville
first interrupted.

"Almy, I am a love-sick fool, and you must
treat me as you would a spoiled child. But tell
me one thing, do you approve of the stand which
Lel has taken against me?"

"I think she is right," replied Mr. Almy.
"You must be well aware that there is no one to
whom I would so gladly yield my daughter as to

you. But I have experienced myself that complete confidence, without which married life is always more or less painful, cannot exist unless the parties practise the same faith. Men may talk as they please about common interests, tastes, and affinities, but a common religion is the only enduring tie. So much for opinion. But our church refuses her blessing to a mixed marriage, and I should be sorry to see Lel make any contract without her benediction."

"It is hard, it is hard," mused Melville.

"I know it is; hard for you and hard for us all; but let us wear the badge of sorrow cheerfully. Since I have been a Catholic I have enjoyed a peace of mind of which you have no conception, and of which I had none. Believe me, Melville, that Young, Shelley, and a host of others were groping after the Catholicity which the Schlegels found, and which Goethe was too proud, Walter Scott too timid to profess. The Catholic Church, in her unchanging grandeur, is worth any man's notice, and I recommend her to your careful study."

Melville was too much excited to sleep. Lel's happiness afflicted him. He wished her miserable to convince him of her love. Yet what could make her happy? Had Catholicity a recompense for every sacrifice it asked? He thought of the change in Mr. Almy; of the change in his face; of his abstinence from old Schiedam; of his tranquil resignation. What had produced it? He thought of Agnes, as he .first saw her, and as she left him; of that strangely beautiful expression, so different from all he had ever seen or fancied. Whence did she obtain it? He thought of Lel's heroic self-denial. Was it sheer fanaticism?

With these questions he easily kept himself awake for hours, and then went to sleep, determining to find out what Agnes meant by the practice of her religion, and what Thomas à Kempis had to say in the chapter on Nature and Grace.

CHAPTER XXV.

OUR story has reached that placid point when a year may be skipped without our missing much incident. Agnes is a pious novice, Lel a sweet country girl, Mr. Almy is regaining his mercantile importance. His fellow-merchants had been civil so long as he needed their assistance, and were courteous when he did not. They could not but respect the industry, honesty, and ability which had almost restored him to his former position. It requires much to reach the point from which Mr. Almy had fallen; it requires much more to regain it. But this accomplished merchant had a fund of dauntless energy which astonished even those who were best acquainted with his resources. No one could tell how he managed to rise so rapidly, but rise he did; and if Catholicity made the ascent more rugged, she doubled his strength, thus lightening the task.

Must we see how Melville studied Catholicity? The converts to our faith, who publish neat little treatises or sweet little novels, the fruits of their experience, are perhaps surprised that the reasons, so convincing to them, are so unsatisfactory to others. Do they ever remember that the grace of God came in some silent, unrecorded moment of humility and contrition, and that their good intentions availed quite as much as their theological researches.

We have seen, in the passage at arms with Mrs. Hoity, that Melville lost his first chance of being a fashionable practitioner. It did not grieve him much; he had never respected the illiterate, ill-bred, low-born, purse-proud aristocracy of his native city, and was glad of an opportunity to meet poverty at home.

He might have been seen one winter night, when Mr. Almy was in bed, seated before his office table, on which medical books and controversial works were piled alternately, like the spots on a chess-board. Melville had long been a free-thinker, and the prejudices of a lifetime are not easily eradicated. Affluence and happiness are very favorable to skepticism, and infidelity had laid a strong hold on him. Nor must we suppose, from his reconciliation with the priest, that he was disposed to accept his kind offer of instruction. Having sufficient pride of intellect and some common sense, that most uncommon of all the senses, he had purchased quite a theological library, in which he was far enough advanced to admit a revelation; still considering *himself* the infallible interpreter.

He was pursuing a treatise on the sufficiency of private judgment when the bell rang. A little girl, poorly clad, was at the door.

"Is your mother worse?" he said.

"Oh, yes, sir; father says she is dying."

Melville took his hat and followed her to a small frame house in an alley. He found the poor woman suffering from extreme nervous excitement after morphine. Having done all he could to calm her, he directed that the utmost silence should be observed, as the least agitation would be fatal.

The little girl whispered to her father, "there's Father John at the door."

"Thank God!" muttered that honest Irishman, whose faith was worthy of the isle that nursed him. Melville's ejaculation was slightly different. He stepped into the front room to meet Father John; and Father John was no other than our friend, the diminutive old priest.

"You cannot see her," whispered Melville.

"Why not ? "

"Because the least excitement will kill her."

"Excitement," said the priest, "I am going to compose, not to excite her."

"I have often witnessed," returned Melville, " the composing effect of religious ceremony on the sick ; it is too apt to compose them into the sleep of death."

"Have you ever known in your experience, Mr. Melville, a patient of yours injuriously agitated by the presence of a Catholic priest?"

"Never," replied Melville, after a pause. "But if other ministers disturb, I do not see how you can fail to annoy."

"We will talk about that another time," and, with this, he was about to enter the chamber when Melville interposed.

"Her life is hanging now by a thread," he muttered; "will you insist on depriving her of her only chance — perfect quiet?"

"She has been a pious woman," said Father John, his eyes flashing as he spoke, "and if her life is hanging by a thread she shall have extreme unction."

"Ay, that she shall," interposed the husband, who, overhearing the conversation, suddenly presented himself. "She shall have it in spite of all the doctors on earth;" and darting a terrible look at Melville as he spoke, the brawny laborer clenched his hands until his finger nails were buried in the palms. Melville, then more alarmed for his patient's sake at the prospect of a fray, resigned himself to the worst.

He saw that poor woman's face lose its anguish as her confessor bent over her; he saw the oil applied, he saw her lips moving in prayer. When the rite was concluded, he felt her pulse, the nervousness had decreased, and before an hour she was asleep. And the good priest smiled to Melville and walked away with him, arm in arm.

From this moment his intimacy with Father John began; and before long he was called upon to witness many such scenes. The arguments for Catholicity are scattered thick around us, not only in books, but in everyday life; and a physician, whose walks are amongst the lower classes, is surely the last who can put in the plea of invincible ignorance. When we behold so many Catholics neglecting their religion, and living year after year out of the church, we are disposed to think that others are kept from joining her rather from love of sin than want of knowledge. And with this remark we leave Melville in the hands of Father John instead of multiplying or repeating reasons, as if it were strange that men become Catholics, and quite natural that they do not.

But Melville was rising in his profession, and already his skill in surgery was mentioned honorably in the first circles. He had only to give up the Catholic Almys and take a seat at the top of the ladder. Or, even with the Almys, for the royal merchant was emerging from the cloud, it might be done if he avoided poor practice. In spite of all these allurements, the young man was blockhead enough never to refuse the petition of poverty, no matter how dangerous, how unprofitable; and this "*grovelling propensity*," as Mrs. Hoity defined his charity, threw a singular light upon his theological researches.

CHAPTER XXVI.

GNES had been nearly two years in the convent; and for two years, Mrs. Cleveland, Lel, and the Colonel have continued to visit the young novice once a week.

Lel and Melville had not met since that morning when the red flag was waving from her window. But she had seen her father often — he had spent whole weeks with her — delicious weeks of rambling, and riding, and love, and joy. The expression he ought to have was indelibly stamped upon his face, and a few days in the country always brought it out in such perfection that she begged him to close his counting-room and turn farmer.

During her walks, she had noticed the progress of a new dwelling-house, built of good, solid logs, handsomely weather-boarded. She heard that a rich gentleman from town was going to live in it, and she often wished that her father had such a home; for when finished it looked so neat and pretty, with its white walls glancing through the cherry-trees around it. And from the porch, which fronted the south, a broad, rich meadow swept down to a green strip of woodland; and above the treetops, on the hills beyond, the yellow grain was waving; and looking to the west, you could see the sunset in the gap of the mountains, and the sun lingered longest there, and the afterglow too. The convent was not in sight, yet it was a beautiful place — the very place Lel would have chosen for her father.

And near it was her favorite retreat, where the running stream had formed a deep pool under the roots of gigantic trees. It was a lovely spot, so shady, so cool, so still. There on the grassy knoll, watching the motionless water-lilies, or reading, or singing, or rolling smooth white pebbles into the clear basin, she seemed to be apart from the rest of the world.

She was sitting there one summer afternoon, thinking of Agnes, who was to take the vows on that day week. Absorbed in thought, she knew not that any human eye was on her — she knew not that a man, tearful and smiling, was standing close behind her, watching her as she twisted the long grass between her fingers, — watching her golden hair as it floated in the wind. She knew not that the moment of all others had come, that in another instant the bright hopes of her youth, which had faded, were to be revived; that her prayer had been heard, that ——

She heard her name pronounced by a voice that made her tremble, and, turning as she started to her feet, saw George Melville before her! He took her cold hand and pressed it to his lips.

"I am a Catholic, Lel," was all he said ; and they knelt together on that green grass and thanked the God who had been so good to them.

And a moment after that prayer of thanksgiving — it *seemed* but a moment — she found herself in the parlor of that new house, pressed to her father's heart. What! could it be! Her own dear, long-lost piano! She flew to it — the lid was raised. One chord!— her heart gave way, and, leaning forward, she wept with her face buried in her arms.

They went to Loretto to spend the night, and the Colonel, though a little jealous of Melville, was the happiest of mortal men, alternately laughing, crying, and coughing, until Mr. Almy suspected his sanity. Mrs. Cleveland testified her pleasure by a blessing full of tenderness and love. And that evening, whilst the Colonel was chatting with Almy, Lel learned from Melville how her medal, Gabriel, and Father John had conquered his stubbornness, — how he had been to confession and received absolution, and how he was permitted to make his first communion with her. He told her that her father had returned him more than half his advances, and had bought the farm and built the house, which he had rented, and which Lel was to name; that he had given up his practice in the city, to spend the rest of his life, if it were the will of heaven, under the shadow of those blue mountains.

And on the porch, between those pillars that could tell of so much joy and pain, it was ordained by our little group of friends that Melville should make his first communion at the convent chapel on the morning Agnes took the vows, and that, after communion, a marriage should be solemnized between George Melville and a certain Ellen Almy.

"So, Lel," said the Colonel, "it has come to this. You are going to give up the old man who has loved you so long for that young scapegrace!"

"And am I not serving you right?" replied Lel. "Did you not know perfectly well that father was building that new house, and that he would be here to-day; and did you not tell George Melville where to find me; and did you not thus permit me to be surprised into saying all sorts of foolish things to him; and after this, are you not a deceitful old dear, not fit to be trusted?

"Ah, Melville, Melville," sighed the Colonel, "from the bottom of my heart I pity you! With a tongue so keen now, what will it be when sharpened on the matrimonial strap?"

"Blunt!" cried Mr. Almy, "if the strap is of the right sort."

And thus, after the first deep calm and silence of reunion, the evening passed playfully away; though under all those glittering bubbles there was a strong current of deep feeling. For how could they help recalling that winter night, when the sleigh stopped at the gate, and the bright Christmas morning that followed, and the long, sweet evenings spent around the crackling wood-fire; and all the changes which had come to pass since then! And how could they help thinking of Agnes, who was no longer there, with her long dark hair, and white temples, and calm, deep, powerful eye.

CHAPTER XXVII.

THE carriage driven by Charlie had left Loretto; the convent bells were ringing for early mass, and Mr. Almy saw Agnes!

As if it were a dream, she advanced from the

Sisters and repeated the words which were to bind her to God. Oh God, how beautiful must the soul be when entering heaven! The plainest face when lit with sanctity is sublime, and prince and peasant bow down before it, or if they smile, it is in envy. No rouge shall ever tinge thy pale cheek, Sister Agnes; no ring shall ever glitter on thy white hand; thy hair shall never be entwined into lockets; thy foot shall never twinkle in the dance! Thou art the child of God, Sister Agnes! And who will dare to claim thee for the world as thou kneelest there before the altar, or say that thou wert made for man? Who would snatch thee hence, thou young companion of the angels, as if thou were to be pitied and saved? *There* is the likeness to God, which the children of earth have lost, and who would bid it vanish?

As if it were a dream, Lel and Melville advanced. They too had made their choice and taken their vows. All had been to communion except the Colonel! A pang went through his heart; he thought of his innocent youth; his sister was next him in prayer, his niece, just consecrated to heaven before him; a young infidel knelt reclaimed and regenerated at his side! Tears of shame burned on his cheeks; he felt separated from all he loved by a terrible abyss.

Repent, old man, thy heart is true, and kind, and warm; repent whilst thou hast time! As the Colonel raised his eyes he saw a stranger on his left; it was Gabriel.

Silently they returned to Loretto; not a word was spoken, unless to welcome Gabriel, when he unexpectedly appeared at the church door to salute the-bride. The day would have hung heavily had it not been for Gabriel. This strange being laughed and sang as he rode along, whilst the rest were in tears; he did not seem to comprehend or to share their depression. And when they reached Loretto his face beamed so brightly, and there was such contagion in his smile, that even the Colonel's brow relaxed.

The afternoon was spent in receiving the congratulations and presents of the neighborhood; presents which Lel, provided by the Colonel's foresight, was able to return with interest.

When the sun was setting in the gap of the mountains they might all have been seen on the porch of the new house. A table was spread in the dining-room with fruits and ices.

"Come, Lel," said Mr. Almy, "it is time to give our local habitation a name."

He drew a decanter from the cooler and wiped the dew-drops from its polished surface.

The glasses were filled and quaffed to Mrs. Melville.

"Now for the name," said the Colonel, replenishing the bride's glass and his own. "Beat Loretto if you can!"

"I cannot beat it, uncle," replied Lel; "I should be glad to equal it. I am not experienced in giving names; and, as I have this morning relinquished my own, I will only suggest a name, which you may reject or adopt at pleasure. Shall it be *Mount Gabriel!*"

"MOUNT GABRIEL!" was echoed with one accord; and Gabriel, little dreaming that he was honored in the name, joined in the applause that hailed the selection, and drained his glass without a blush.

After a sufficient time had elapsed to admire the name which Lel had chosen, and to wish all imaginable peace and happiness to Mount Gabriel, Melville, pressing a fair hand that was resting in his, and looking at Gabriel, who sat next the Colonel, said, with a full heart and brimming eye:—

"There is one who must not be forgotten to-night, and but for whom I should not have the treasure I now possess. Father John! May God reward that blameless priest!"

"Charlie!" whispered the Colonel.

The boy stooped and drew a black bottle from a cooler, which, unnoticed by Mr. Almy, he had placed at his master's side.

"I kept this bottle for another marriage," said the Colonel, "and it is worthy of this. Forty years has it lain in my cellar, the last representative of a noble stock. I have looked upon it as my own blood, as the liquid that kept kept me alive; and when it is gone I know that I must soon follow. However, the time has come! Charlie, bring the glasses!"

With a trembling hand the old man inclined the bottle in silence, that was only broken by the gurgling and trickling of the wine. When every glass was jewelled to the rim, he rose and leaned upon the back of his chair.

"I kept this bottle for another marriage," he began; "it cannot fulfil its destiny. Yet"—the glass shook and ran over in his hand—"yet I have kept it for one, and to *her* must it still be pledged. I propose the memory of"——

"Sister Agnes!" said Mr. Almy, as the Colonel, unable to utter the name, applied the glass to his lips. They rose in silence and sympathy—"*Sister Agnes!*"

Before ten o'clock the new house had heard all about the past, and began to feel like a home: the chairs and matting looked nearly as kind and knowing as the old piano, which gave tone to everything around it.

"Our cup of happiness is full," said Mr. Almy, "and you might search the earth without finding a family in possession of that peace and confidence we now enjoy. But there is one to whose happiness ours is nothing. Could we see the heart of Sister Agnes, blessed as we are, we might envy her."

He was right. That depression, that spiritual desolation had passed away; that calm delight and loving trust had come; the aspirations of her young soul had been fulfilled, ay, more than fulfilled; she was sleeping the smiling sleep of baptismal innocence under the eye of God.

"What an argument for the church was in her face this morning," said Melville. "And I am now convinced," he whispered in Lel's ear, "*that I was seeking Catholicity when I sought Agnes.*"

The Colonel rose to go, Gabriel to accompany him. The old man had a necklace for Lel, more beautiful than the first, and as he threw it around her neck, he kissed her glowing forehead.

"Is she not a daughter to be proud of," said Mr. Almy, drawing her to his side. "Oh, my dear Lel, if all our Catholic girls had faith and firmness enough to follow your example; or, if they were only taught to prefer an humble match in the church to a brilliant alliance out of it, how much misery would they escape, and how many a precious soul be saved!"

Good-night! The Colonel departed, followed by Charlie and Gabriel.

CHAPTER XXVIII.

R. Almy did not remain long in possession of Mount Gabriel. Soon after her marriage Lel discovered a deed in her drawer, making her absolute mistress of the property.

"It would never do," he said, "for me to be the master of the house while Melville is master of you. We should be at sixes and sevens before many months. All I want is a good room when I come to see you; for, mind, you'll have quite as much of me as you care to have."

"Upon my word, sir," remonstrated Melville, "our calculation was to have you always with us."

"And we'll have more fights without you than with you, won't we, Melville?"

"God bless you both; but it can't be yet. You keep the country-house, and I'll keep the town-house; give me your winters and I'll give you my summers, or as much of them as I can spare from business."

"Oh, hang business, pa, haven't you had enough of it, and money enough, too, for any sensible man? If you keep on with business you'll be an old miser yet."

"Well, suppose I am, if it's all for your sake?"

"No one ever makes money for one's own sake," said Lel, smiling. "It's always for somebody else's sake."

Mr. Almy laughed, and took her hand.

"You may live to see me a rope-dancer or a politician, but you'll never live to see me a miser. I'm too young to stop business; I should rust and mope here amongst your milk and meadows, and get tired even of your mountains. There's nothing so hard on an old merchant as the country when administered in large doses. Literary men can stand it; physicians can stand it; I am even told that lawyers can sometimes stand it; but with merchants it's invariably fatal. I never knew of an instance to the contrary. So I don't mean to make a mummy of myself, even for you and Melvillé."

When farther pressed by Lel alone he still held his ground.

"You can hardly comprehend," he would say,

"how a merchant loves his house. It is both his mother and his child; they exist only through each other. We have been through many a gale together; once, as you know, we nearly sank; but we are having smooth seas and fine winds now, and it would be silly to give up the ship just as the promise of the voyage is brightening. I think it a just ambition to excel in any honorable career. A few years will more than make my house what it was before—you sold your piano. And then, Lel, if I were to turn farmer now it would puzzle me to pay off Melville."

"What a poor excuse, father," answered Lel; "you have paid him nearly all as it is."

"And am quite able, with a very little effort, to pay what remains. Suppose he were to turn out a ruffian, and beat you before my eyes! How could I ever knock him down with a clean conscience if I owed him money? No, darling, I'm not saint enough to owe a cent to a son-in-law when I have it in my power to stand square. Nor am I sinner enough ever to pain you by falling back into any of my old habits. And since Agnes has turned nun there's little danger of my ever relapsing into married life. Are you satisfied now, or do you still doubt me, my bright-eyed unbeliever?"

Lel looked very sad and uncertain. But pressently a dreamy light stole into her eyes like a melody — one of her old inspirations. A strange swift smile passed over her face, followed by a blush, swift and strange as the smile. Both blush and smile were new to her father.

"You ought to know best," she said, turning away, "at all events I find *my* influence over you at an end."

The sharp accent on *my* was unlike Lel, but Mr. Almy thought no more of it at the time.

And so the autumn parted them. Mr. Almy took rooms in town, and they saw no more of him till Christmas. He was a week with them then, but more or less restless and anxious to be back at his desk. He was doing an enormous and prosperous business. No one knew how rich he was, but the knowing ones all said that Almy was making money very fast. He certainly spent it very fast, for almost as fast as he made it it was transferred to Lel. Before spring he had paid off all his obligations to Melville, with interest. Lel could scarcely take up a newspaper without observing some allusion to his prosperity and public charities. But instead of making her happy it made her afraid. She had long, loving letters from him once or twice a week, but it did not satisfy her. She was afraid to trust him alone in the world. He needed daily love and care and domestic beauty to fill his heart and absorb all other craving. She determined to see for herself how he was behaving, and spend part of the winter with him if she could accomplish it. It was a little difficult, inasmuch as Melville, having just been employed as physician to the convent, could not well accompany her. But, as there were no longer any secrets between them, he would accede at once to any leave of absence she might ask.

So when Mr. Almy paid them the Christmas visit it happened that Lel wanted a hundred things from town which she had never thought of before, and which he could not possibly send; things which men know nothing about, and which women only are competent to buy.

"In fact," she said, "although you're slow about inviting me, pa, I'll run down with you, for a week or so, if you'll give me a room next yours at the hotel."

He was delighted, as every father is whose daughter leaves her husband behind to go off with *him*, and they went away together. She was happy, too, in returning more distinctly to the old sacred relationship again, and did not at all reproach herself for being a spy in disguise. On the contrary, she consoled herself in having made many important discoveries. He was even richer than she thought. Some bold and vast adventures had been terribly lucrative, and made him more than ever the first merchant of the city. He had become, for the first time in his life, very fond of dress. He was growing handsomer as he grew older. He kept a carriage and fast horses. He saw very little of Father John. His apartments were superbly furnished; one of them to her horror was a card-room.

The night after her arrival quite a number of her father's old friends came dropping in. At first she thought it very kind of them to call on her so soon, very kind indeed. But when, after some little fidgeting and hesitancy, the card-table was brought out, and she found herself gradually forgotten in the game, her eyes were opened to the true state of the case. This scared her more than anything else. It was a new feature. He had never cared for cards before. It was a late development and therefore a dangerous one. Follies at his age are fatal. What was to be done? She must act at once, now or never. Her clear duty as a lady was to retire forthwith, and leave the enemy in possession of the field. It was evidently expected of her — she was a drag on the game, an obstacle to all honest betting. Some of the veterans already began to eye her viciously and exchange winks. Unfortunately the game was not whist; it was a rapid, five-card game, quite new to her, with what they called a "pool" in the middle. It was a game in which she could not with any propriety ask for a hand; it was not by any means a ladies' game; she had not the shadow of an excuse for staying. But stay she did, in spite of sundry imploring glances from her father. They might throw her out of the window, it was very likely they would; but she would never leave by the door. The game closed at twelve with a supper. It was one before she and Mr. Almy were alone with each other.

"Gracious goodness," said Lel, "do you mean to keep me up this late every night?"

"Which means," replied Almy, smiling, "that you will do your best every night to spoil my card-party?"

"*I* spoil your card-party," exclaimed this young innocent. "When did *I* ever spoil any sport of yours in my life? It's too late to begin now. If your friends object to my looking on, I'll find some other way to amuse myself; but as to going to bed before *you* in this big, lonely house, to be robbed or murdered, I won't do it. I'd go home at once and be out of the way if the dentist was only done with me!"

Mr. Almy laughed. It seemed as if the dentist would never be done with her, so many of her teeth wanted fixing.

"It's no laughing matter," she gravely continued, "to live fifty miles away from a decent dentist. And I intend having my mouth put in perfect order if it takes a year."

She was trying hard to be very angry; but her father saw through the whole conspiracy. He crossed his hands and laid back in his chair with the air of a man resigning himself to his fate.

"I never knew the day," he said, "when your mouth was *not* in perfect order. Kiss me and go to bed."

"Good night, pa. I trust that I'll not be in the way to-morrow night."

He did not exactly know what to make of her. Would she leave him to his little amusements in peace, and retreat in offended dignity? It was not like her. She most probably had a masked battery somewhere in reserve. But what would it avail her against his banded veterans? They were too many and too strong for her. He was determined to remain neutral and keep his temper if he could. It was very impertinent of her to interfere, but she was doing it for his own good. A man could not stand late suppers and

late play forever. But when one is obliged to
create a home without wife or child after one
has lived long with both, one surely has a right
to make it as jolly as possible. It is somewhat
provoking to be dictated to by a daughter who
is having her own way in her own house, and
who is jealously averse to having a rich father
incline to anything or anybody else. But he
would keep his temper until driven to the wall,
and then bring Lel to her senses with a word.
Meanwhile he was curious to see how she would
contrive not to be in the way at their next ses-
sion.

After dinner the next day they went to
the card-room together. Lel begged not to have
the gas lit, so they sat and talked in the beautiful twilight — talked over old times, and Mrs.
Hoity, and Sister Agnes, until, one by one, the
same set began to drop in and the room was
lighted. Then, for the first time, Mr. Almy observed an addition to the furniture. Lel had
ordered a piano on trial; her old one was wearing out at last; Chickering's grands were said
to be so much better than hers. It was a noble
instrument, and stood pretty well out in the room
so as to have its finger-board well under the action of the gasolier. She had also bought a
quantity of new music to play over for Melville,

and it lay menacingly on the card-table. But
she swept it away as soon as the gentlemen appeared, and, after exchanging compliments with
them, began to try it over with the soft pedal
down. She had kept her word, and found some
other way to amuse herself, as she had promised.
This was her masked battery.

She touched the keys very lightly at first —
just a note here and there — a little spirit of
melody and then silence. She seemed disposed
to respect the sanctity of their game; she would
doubtless go to bed soon. But two of the principal players were two of her oldest adorers; they
had petted her when she was a child, and made
her sing and play for them as soon as she could
strike an octave or turn a tune. They were two
bachelor brothers, very fond of good living and
good music — very fond of cards, too, subordin-
ately. Lel remembered perfectly that Sam, the
elder, had a weakness for "God save the King."
He considered "God save the King" the greatest mortal composition. He could whistle a
light opera through after one hearing, but he
stuck to "God save the King" for all that.
After trifling with her new music an hour or
more she threw it aside and began to improvise.
She began a very long way from the English
anthem, but Sam instantly pricked up his ears —

he scented the melody afar off. He looked once or twice askant at his Brother Barnard. Now and then a dreamy suggestion of the strain came sweeping by in a swift, smothered minor, and Sam was all at sea, mistook too pairs for a full, and got well laughed at in the bargain; but Barnard, although he controlled himself better, got nervous too, and forgot to pass the knife and *anti*, much to the disgust of several ancient gentlemen who could not account for such absurd behavior. Presently, however, the full phrase was enunciated, and Lel carried the theme straight and simply through with her left hand. Then all was chaos again, with a vague purpose glimmering through it — with only a feeble, broken spiral of sunshine on the troubled waters. And then a grand let-there-be-light prelude, as she swept the scale with both hands, lashing the powerful instrument into orchestral fury, and looking herself like an inspired priestess of song. After much coughing and choking, after several suppressed indications of joining in the air, after manifold fatal discardings, and serious losses, Sam threw down his hand and burst in with the words at the top of his voice. They tried to stop him, but it was no use; he went through to the end.

The veterans were indignant; but they were

gentlemen of the old school, and could overlook a single indiscretion.

"It shan't occur again," apologized Sam; "though the girl plays like an angel. Play something else, Lel; keep that for some other time; I can stand anything but that."

Barnard said nothing, but catching Lel's eye, winked aside at her. The intimation was needless. Lel had anticipated his desire. He was as much wrapped up in "Annie Laurie" as Sam in "God save the King." She approached the air remotely. Barnard's ear was subtler than Sam's. She tormented him with hope deferred, long before any of the others suspected what she was about. He was tender-hearted, and the tears were in his eyes every now and then as if he had a cold. He was unmanned long before she reached the air; his hand trembled as he sipped his whisky and water; his voice was thin and husky; he finally begged them to go on without him, and went and sat by the piano, listening contentedly to the beautiful air, and looking way back through the mists of the past to a fond face that was gone forever; to the white hand from which he had taken the thin gold ring still worn on his finger.

Supper was ordered earlier than usual, and did not last as long.

"I say, Almy," mumbled one of the oldsters, at parting, "we'll have to drop our game till your nightingale goes back to her mountains. There's no use of our trying to play against her."

"Nonsense, man," said Almy, "we'll make these silly brothers behave themselves better to-morrow."

But the silly brothers could not be coaxed or bullied into behaving any better, and Lel could not be induced to give up her music.

"I must do *something* to amuse myself, or I shall die," she said to her father. "But you'll be rid of me as soon as my teeth 'are fixed."

The result was that one by one the card-party diminished, until Sam and Barnard were the only survivors.

"Now, pa," cried Lel, when she first found themselves reduced to four, "let's have whist, and I'll bet as high as you like."

So, ever after that, as long as Lel stayed in town they had their whist and music, instead of bluff and supper, and Mr. Almy got to like it quite as well. If she could only have kept her ground, those routed veterans could never have reassembled in force. As it was, she feared, and with too much reason, that as soon as her back was turned the whole jolly set would be back in force. *How* she would pray for him! How she would set Sister Agnes to pray for him! And, all the while, a bright hope in the distance went through her heart like a ceaseless song.

CHAPTER XXIX.

DURING Lel's visit to her father a stranger had come to Mount Gabriel. A beautiful boy, with light hair and blue eyes. It was Clarence. Lel remembered him at sight, but wondered how he came there. Melville had kept the track of the Wanderer. It was the only secret not yet confided to his wife. Professional lies are said to be very venial, and generally very successful. Yet it was in vain that he sought to evade her questions by pleading a vague interest in the youth and his musical father. The neighbors, including the household of Loretto, were content to accept the boy as a patient entrusted to the superior skill of Dr. Melville. And Clarence's appearance gave color to the story. His life of privation and exposure had been too much for him. The shadow of the other world was on his youth, and not even the skill of Dr. Melville could remove it.

Lel was maturing into a diplomatist. She perceived that her husband was hiding something from her, and felt it her solemn duty to nip all such insane proceedings in the bud.

"A charming boy," she kept saying, "but who is he?"

"Why, don't you remember, Lel, that poor chorus singer and his son?"

"Certainly, I remember. But who is the chorus singer?"

"Why, the Wanderer, of course — the man who interested me so much in London. He seems to think he has some claim on me."

"Indeed. Corresponds with you occasionally, I presume."

"Occasionally."

"Do you know his present address? "

"I know what his *future* address will soon be. The same as his son's."

"You mean *the grave*," said Lel, wincing, and almost silenced.

"Exactly," said Melville, "I mean the grave."

"But, doctor, pursued Lel, rallying, "if the dear boy should die on our hands it would be awkward to bury him without knowing his last name. *Has* he any last name?"

Melville smiled. His solemnity had failed to repulse her. And why, after all, should there

be any mystery between them? His promise of
secrecy to the Wanderer was made as a bachelor, not as a married man. And, moreover, she
had a clear right to know. Since she had driven
him into a corner it was wiser to surrender
without a battle than with one. It was only
from his instinctive and inveterate reticence
that he had hesitated to enlighten her.

"You know, Melville," she resumed, "if anything happens I'd like to pray for him by his
last name as well as his first, if only to prevent
mistakes."

"Can't you guess his last name?"

"Indeed I can't," she said, after a moment's
reflection.

"Do you see no likeness between him and a
friend of yours?"

Clarence had grown more like Agnes than
ever, but Lel did not catch the resemblance;
the color of the hair and eyes was different.

"A friend of mine?"

"Of yours and mine. Really, Lel, you have
less penetration than I gave you credit for. I
may well get obstinate when my wife grows
stupid."

Her eyes were opened at last. It all flashed
upon her like lightening. The figure of the
Wanderer had lost its significance in the two

eventful intervening years; the bitter story was one which a pure woman's heart is ever the last to realize, but she could be blind to its full meaning no longer. She grew pale as death as she hesitatingly asked : —

"Do you mean that his name is Cleveland?"

"Yes." And he rose to leave the room.

"Stay awhile," said Lel. "Does Sister Agnes know of this?"

"No. Do you think she ought to?"

"Where is the Wanderer?" He told her.

"Has he recovered health? Is he well?"

"From Clarence's account, and his own, he can scarcely survive this winter. In fact, I should not be surprised at any moment to hear the worst."

"Gracious heaven, Melville, what a pretty Catholic you are. You converts never seem to think of saving any souls but your own, except controversially. The man must see his daughter, and see her at once; she may save him."

"They won't let her go, will they?" asked the bewildered physician.

"Won't let her go!" repeated Lel, in loving scorn." "She'll be *sent* there to-morrow morning."

"Then you want the carriage ordered?"

"Immediately."

"Am I to accompany you?"

"No. No one but Clarence. Order the light wagon. I'll drive myself."

"Has your ladyship any more orders before her departure?"

"Yes. Never keep anything from your wife again. The sooner men learn this lesson the better."

In a very few minutes more Lel was driving Clarence to the convent. She asked to see the Mother Superior, and leaving the boy in the parlor was shown into the adjoining room. It did not take her long to explain, nor did it take the Mother long to decide. A sister servant was going south in the morning, and Sister Agnes could go with her. It would answer exactly. Would Mrs. Melville like to see Sister Agnes now? The Mother would bring her.

Lel returned to the parlor, where they were soon joined by Sister Agnes and the Superior.

Agnes started at the sight of Clarence. She knew him at once, and took a seat beside him, saying, —

"So we have met again, my young friend. Don't you remember me?"

He gazed at her with a puzzled expression.

"Have you forgotten the lady who used to give you pineapples and oranges?"

He knew her then.

"Is it *you?*" exclaimed the boy, and burst into tears. "I've never forgotten you, night or day. I've looked for your face wherever we went, for it seemed to follow us in all our travels. I thought, perhaps, you were in heaven, and all the while you were a nun."

"Which is nearly the same thing," said Lel.

"Where is your father?" asked Agnes.

"Somewhere in the south with the Company."

"Does he still sing?"

"When he can."

"Is he no better?"

"I am afraid not, but Dr. Melville can tell you."

"Why did he part with you?"

"He said the life was too hard on me."

"Are you sick yourself?"

"Sometimes," said Clarence, smiling.

"And, if our Lord wills it," said the Mother, "you would not mind His taking you where you thought He had already taken Sister Agnes, would you, Clarence?"

"Not if He'd take us both together," replied Clarence, with amusing simplicity.

"Why, the little Wanderer," laughed Lel, though tears were for an instant in the eyes of all of them. "I fear your poor father will be the first to leave us," she resumed, more seriously. "His last letter to Dr. Melville was dated from the hospital."

"Then it is not unlikely that Sister Agnes may soon see him," said the Mother.

Agnes looked up with the subdued, resigned curiosity of a Sister.

"She starts on her first mission to-morrow with Sister Seraphine," continued the Mother, "and as their way lies south they may possibly come across your father."

"I hope so," murmured Clarence. "He remembers her as well as I do. He is always talking about Mr. Melville's sister."

"Mr. Melville's sister!" exclaimed the Mother.

"A delirious reminiscence," explained Lel, "occasioned by the fever through which they nursed him."

Sister Agnes sat like a statue, her eyes on the ground, and a smile on her lips.

"I will show Clarence over the house myself," resumed the Mother, rising, "while you two old friends say good-by to each other. Come, Clarence."

Lel and Agnes walked out into the open air. It was a bright, warm, February day, "a straggler from the files of June." The gravelled walks were hard and dry. The two friends could talk better with no walls around them, and only the blue sky above them. They could see Loretto, too, on the mountain side, and there was a charm in that, a common point for both their hearts to rest on.

"My poor uncle will never get over my being a Sister," said Agnes. "The greatest trial I now have is in remembering the pain I caused him. Pray for him, Lel, he is so good and noble."

"On one condition, Agnes — that you pray for my father."

"I always pray for him," said Agnes, while her cheek flushed ever so little.

"But pray twice as hard," insisted Lel. "He's in the hands of a set of Philistines, who threaten to bind him hand and foot, and would have done so but for me."

Agnes laughed.

"It's no laughing matter, Sister Agnes Cleveland, and if you don't pray your best for him he'll go back to his old habits. He's no longer fit to take care of himself; that's the plain fact. At his age fathers are only fit to be grandfathers."

Agnes was gazing intently at Loretto. She did not notice the crimson blush which flashed from Lel's cheeks, as if she had said more than she meant to.

"Clarence is dying," said Agnes, without removing her eyes from Loretto. "He will never see his father again."

"But *you* will."

"I know it. It is for that I am sent with dear Sister Seraphine."

"How do you know?"

Agnes smiled the old smile of the past, and threw her arm around her cousin as in days gone by.

"How do I know everything?" she answered. "Is it so hard to interpret the kindness of our noble Mother, and the officiousness of little Ellen Almy? Ah, Lel, your touch is a golden one; I should know it in ten thousand. But here comes our Mother with Clarence. She has been telling him of heaven."

It was true. The boy had of course been enchanted with the loveliness of the place, and the Mother had of course improved the opportunity by instilling into his mind the superior glories of the after-world. The Mother excelled in preaching these little sermons. She knew how to carry every word straight to the heart. She lived so much in God herself that she had little difficulty in bringing others home to Him. Lel had never seen him look so sweet and happy.

"You must say good-by, now," said the Mother, "for Sister Agnes will have to work hard to get off."

"Don't make her mission a long one, Mother," said Lel. "Good-by, Agnes."

"Good-by, Lel. And you, Clarence, remember all our dear Mother has said to you. Most likely we shall never meet again on earth, but you will soon have better faces than mine to follow you. Pray for Sister Agnes, and she will pray for you. If I meet your father I'll take care of him as though he were my own."

Lel watched her like a hawk, as these last words were uttered, to see if her manner or accent betrayed any deeper consciousness of their significance; but Agnes was impenetrable. There was nothing to discern more than the simple promise of a good Sister of Charity.

Clarence wept so he could not speak, and in spite of Agnes' resistance kissed her hand at parting. He was silent all the way home, and only smiled when Gabriel rushed out to help Lel to the ground.

"It is upward, not downward, you desire to go," whispered Gabriel, as he held her poised a moment in the air. "Never mind, you will go there yet." And he led her into the house with the triumph of a guardian angel in escort of a soul that's saved.

"How's Sister Agnes?" cried Melville, from his office.

"Very well. She starts on her first mission to-morrow, as I told you," she added, as he appeared.

"Then I'll have to forgive your keeping dinner waiting." And George Melville humbly and silently thanked heaven for having given him the hand of Ellen Almy.

CHAPTER XXX.

AR to the South, a thousand miles away from Loretto, at the single window of his chamber, sat the Wanderer watching the people passing carelessly below. Little thought they of the grave to which he was hastening. The spring of that soft climate has already begun, but he will never see the summer. He is emaciated almost to a shadow. He has fought manfully for life, but it is leaving him. His thoughts are not of the city around him, or even of the world beyond this; they are with the boy who may survive him, with the distant inmates of Loretto.

As the sun set a Sister entered with the evening meal. This was not the Sister who had hitherto served 'him, but a stranger. It was the same to him; he scarcely looked at her, although she seemed to linger longer around the table than others did. Only once their eyes met, and had the light been stronger he must have seen her cheek whiten and her eye dilate. But when she left the room her face remained with him, and began to connect itself with another face, ever present in his mind. Her strange emotion strengthened the likeness. Surely he had seen her before — but where? The red spot on his cheek deepened; in vain he strove to calm himself; his hand shook as he raised the untasted cup to his lips. There must have been some powerful memories at work within that wasted frame to nerve it so! He started up, rang the bell, and when Agnes reappeared, the invalid, who had crept to his chair, was pacing the room with a firm, steady step.

"Tell me, Sister," he began, holding the light to her face, "have I not seen you before? Were you not Miss Melville?"

"You mistook my name, sir," replied Agnes; "it is not Melville, but Cleveland; Agnes Cleveland."

The word had frozen him. He clutched her wrist; then reeling back would have fallen but for her quick support.

She guided him to his bed. His hand was still on her wrist, he spoke not, he scarcely seemed to breathe, but kept gazing into her eyes, as if he had not power to end the long, fixed, terrible look.

Oh heaven, how her young heart throbbed! Will he not end that awful silence and call her — "*Daughter?*" "Father!" the word was trembling on her lips; she read the secret in his eye. She was leaning forward; she felt his breath on her cheek; she had almost touched his marble forehead! He turned from her with a groan, and, dropping her hand, buried his face in the pillow.

Then came a fearful doubt across her mind — he might not be her father!

She turned her face away; she pressed her hand against her heart; she signed the cross on her breast, and stood upright awhile, motionless as a statue. She had not power to move, such was the recoil of disappointed hope; until, gathering all her strength, she broke the spell, as a river breaks its fetters of ice. One glance more at that prostrate, deathlike figure, and she walked hastily towards the door.

"Agnes! Agnes!" She turned. The voice went thrilling to her soul. She saw the Wanderer bending towards her, his arms flung wide to receive her. Trembling and murmuring, her hands clasped and straining, she shrank cowering back against the wall. The figure danced before her eyes; it seemed as if she could never reach those outstretched arms, an iron chain seemed to hold her back.

"Agnes! Agnes! behold your father!" One wild leap brought her to his bosom! And at last she said the word — "*Father! Father!*"

CHAPTER XXXI.

THE night had passed — the morning sun was shining.

"Yes, my child," said Mr. Cleveland, "I was once as good and guiltless as you are now. At college I was noted for piety — my sole ambition was to be a good priest. To this, however, my parents would not listen, and I was forced into society. At first I loathed, at last I loved it. I became enamored of a young lady who had no wealth, and whose pretensions were inferior to mine. I wished to marry her, but my parents sternly forbade the match, and I had reverence enough left to obey them."

He paused for breath; it required all her attention to keep pace with the deep meaning he poured into every word.

"Your grandfather and your grandmother were good, worthy people; but, as I had some little eloquence, they wished me to shine at the bar. They were fashionable Catholics, and did not care to have their son a priest. But remember, Agnes, I was more to blame in resigning than they in opposing my vocation."

He smiled — it was the first smile she had ever seen on his face. "Thank God! you are a Sister of Charity," he said, running his eye over her black habit.

"Well," he resumed, "your mother" — he bent his head reverently at the name — "was selected as a proper person for me, though a few years older, and I was married to her at twenty-four. During the few years we lived happily together I contrived to abandon my profession, spend my fortune, and fall in debt. Your uncle, the Colonel, was my fast friend in all financial difficulties, and so loaded me with obligations that I hated him. Agnes, before I proceed, let me say that no human love can content the soul that, called to give itself entirely to God, refuses; it wanders on unsatisfied forever."

And this was the truth which Mr. Almy could not reach, when he styled himself in the neighborhood of a hidden truth. A change came over the Wanderer's face — he no longer looked at

his child — and turned away from her as he
continued : —

"I found that I was still loved by the poor
girl whom I unwillingly deserted; and I ceased
to love your mother, pure and beautiful as she
was. I made no secret of my aversion, and was
unmoved by her grief, her gentleness, her dignity.
I was steeled even against your infant smiles and
caresses

"Your uncle, who had patiently endured my
contempt of him, was maddened by my heartless
treatment of his sister; and once when I insulted
her in his presence, before I could defend myself,
he felled me with his cane. Here is the scar,"
he said, lifting his black hair from his temple,
and Agnes remembered Melville's song and her
mother's groan.

"That blow sealed my fate! I will not ask
you, my pure, noble girl, to follow me through
my dark career of ingratitude and crime. It
will be read against me where all the living and
the dead shall hear it ! "

. He threw her arms from his neck.

"Oh God ! " he said, "that I should suffer this
young innocent to approach me! Agnes, my
lips are steeped in blasphemy, and I have let you
kiss them ; my head is bent with curses, and I
have let you press it to your bosom ; my hands

are red with iniquity, and you have held them;
I am an outcast, and you call me father!"

He shuddered as he spoke.

"There is but one redeeming trait to plead
for me in the ear of God, and that is Clarence.
For him I relinquished the delight of death and
despair. I taught him his prayers, I counter-
feited virtue, that he might never look on vice,
and I sent him away—I yielded up my child
that he might not know my dark and bitter
end."

Agnes trembled, but she saw a solitary tear
start from his eye, and in that single drop there
was comfort and hope!

"Why should I wish to be saved?" he cried.
"It would be asking too much of heaven! I
have been tempted lately to see if life will last
me to Loretto, that I might again behold your
mother. I know she would receive me—I
know she would save me—but it is too much
blessedness!"

"Father!" whispered Agnes, but he was not
listening.

"Oh, Mary!" he said, "instead of branding me
as a traitor you have been filling heaven with
prayers for me; you have offered up your virtues, like sweet victims, for my sins; you have
trained my daughter for her God; you have

permitted her to love and embrace me; you have devoted your life to save me!"

"And not in vain!" cried Agnes, not in interrogation or entreaty, but in exulting accents of confidence and command, as, rising to her full height, she caught his hand, and, pointing to the crucifix on the wall, repeated,—

"Not in vain, my father!"

He was awed by the sublimity of her attitude and expression. She had assumed his repentance, and the impossibility of it no longer occurred.

"You are young and sinless," he said; "you know not how suffering and guilt, how years of sorrow received and inflicted, how scorn and hatred, and want and woe, and crime, can harden the heart."

"But I know," returned Agnes, "that heaven is merciful, and that its grace can penetrate the hardest heart, and that you have been penitent for years. Oh, my dear, long-lost father," she continued, falling at his feet; "when I first heard that you lived, and when your image returned from oblivion—when mother and I were weeping together, she promised that we should *all meet in heaven*, and I dried my tears and believed it. Tell me, father, shall it not be so? can you disappoint her without one effort to gratify?"

That proud lip quivered an instant; and then, and not till then, in the agony and rapture of repentance that followed, had Agnes truly found her father.

  .   .   .   .

They are journeying to the North—two Sisters and the Wanderer. Agnes had conquered—he had tasted the Lamb that redeems the world,—he was on his way to Loretto. But will he reach it? His face is wan and wasted, his shrunken limbs scarcely sustain his weight; hour after hour that fatal cough, that incessant drain on life, continues. He makes no moan, no murmur, but humbly and patiently sits beside his child, hearing the story of her life, or filling up the outlines of his own. And as Agnes listened, and watched his bright, splendid eye, and beautiful head, she saw what power and strength had once been lodged in that crumbling wreck of genius and virtue.

They are half way to Loretto. Oh, will he reach it? Alas, the Wanderer is in his berth—he can no longer sit on deck beside his child; it oppresses him to speak—he can only smile and look at her. How could he endure the jolting stage and racking car?

There was strong will and strong hope within that wasted frame.

"Oh, God!" he prayed, "grant me life, that I

may see her once more, that I may hear the voice of pardon from her lips. I ask it not for my sake, but for hers! Let me see her again; let her see that her life of prayer has not been in vain; let her hear me bless her with my last breath!"

The grace of God, and the determination to live, kept him alive.

CHAPTER XXXII.

THE world had changed for Clarence. It was no longer either a prison or a play-ground. His privations and pastimes were both at an end. He knew that he was to die. Sister Agnes and the Mother had intimated it too clearly for misapprehension. Although reconciled to his lot, he could not escape the consciousness of submission. It saddened and haunted him. He would sit dreaming over his books, listening to Lel's music, with tears in his eyes, and a far-off gaze into futurity. He sought the quietest corners of the house where he could sit or kneel alone. For the fields and the flowers he had ceased to care; his chief earthly love was for the mountains, their misty summits and shaded gorges. He longed to be upon them, to peer beyond them. They lay like a barrier between him and the unknown region toward which he was drifting. He longed to sail with the clouds, above them, behind them. He was glad when day was over and the stars came out, each with its golden declaration that there were other worlds — millions of others — besides this.

When Gabriel was not with the Colonel he was with Clarence. Much as the boy was attached to Lel and Melville, he clung most to Gabriel. For Gabriel knew such beautiful prayers, and could tell such charming legends of saints and hermits, and talk of angels until their white wings seemed to rustle in the room; and he knew how to picture heaven so very brightly that the crystal doors appeared wide open as he spoke. He was seldom sad when Gabriel was with him. And when Gabriel discovered his wish to be among the mountains, and saw he had not strength to walk there, he begged from Lel, too glad to give it, her little wagon. Day after day they drove from slope to slope, from gap to gap, from spring to spring; and day after day Clarence would expect some other landscape to open at his feet, some glimpse at least of the fair fields of the hereafter.

More than once on their rambles they stopped at Loretto. But Mrs. Cleveland, so gentle to all else, seemed stern with Clarence. Once, when he chanced to clasp her hand, she shrank from

him as if a serpent stung her.   And the look she
gave him made Clarence wonder, and ask Gabriel what it meant.

"If you were to live," said Gabriel, " you would
meet many such looks."

" From her ? "

" From all."

" Then, it is better to die ? "

" Our Father in heaven seems to think so."

" What have I done to deserve such looks ? "

" You ? Nothing."

" Who, then ? "

" Your father."

" My father ! — Clarence only knew his father
as an invalid and benefactor ; as the guardian who
had instructed him for first communion and confirmation ; as a lonely, uncomplaining martyr.
The idea of his father's having done any wrong,
or, more than all, of having brought shame upon
his son, was something incomprehensible and
monstrous. "My father ! " was all the boy could
say.

" Why should I reveal a story that your own
eyes will soon read without help of mine," said
Gabriel. "And yet ——. Do you remember
your mother, Clarence ? "

" I was too young to remember her. I remember her picture."

" Was her picture like Mrs. Cleveland ? "

"Oh, no. They are very different."

"And yet Mrs. Cleveland is your father's wife."

The boy was silent. He sat in a maze. A sudden gleam of light overspread the past, and made all plain that had been obscure. What had he to live for *now?* *Why* had he ever wished to live? And suddenly the grave, from which he had shrunk, grew beautiful. For he remembered, even in Lel, a strange reserve at times, and a faltering more than once when she stooped to kiss him; and there was a deliberate pity in Mr. Melville's glance which was now accounted for. He felt and comprehended all. He blessed God in his heart for taking him from a world in which he was misplaced. And then a horrible fear crept over him like a chill. Would God and the angels look coldly on him too? In his sudden panic he clung trembling to his companion's arm.

"It will make no difference *there*, will it Gabriel?"

"Not more than it makes with me," said Gabriel, clasping the child to his heart. And had one passed them then, he would have taken it for one angel embracing another.

There was one peak which they had not yet visited — the highest. Clarence had often begged to go there, but Gabriel was afraid of overtasking him; for it involved a little climbing afoot as

well as a long drive. But one afternoon, a
month or more after Agnes' departure, he was
so bent upon going there that Gabriel yielded,
not without misgiving, although the boy seemed
brighter and stronger. Clarence sang as they
passed the graveyard and the church on the hill.
He was on his way at last to the purple, thunder-
riven rocks of which he had heard so much. He
would see at last where the sun set, and his eye
flashed and his cheek brightened at the thought.

They tied Lel's pony beneath the huge bould-
ers that formed the summit. Gabriel would
have carried him up the steep, but the boy
sprang before him as if he had never known
either sadness or fatigue, and stood gazing at
the sun, which was opening through the nearest
gorge a pathway of purple and scarlet, and shining around himself in a wide aureola of glory.
He was holding communion with something he
saw, something visible to him alone, and he
spoke not even to Gabriel. But Gabriel standing beside him knew the sign, and whispered: —

"Are they calling you?"

The boy's lips grew crimson, a crimson deeper
than the sunset, a crimson that fell at last in
drops at his feet. And this was his only answer.

"This is sudden," said Gabriel, lifting him in
his arms. "Look for it as we may, it is sure to
make us tremble when it comes."

"It does not make me tremble, Gabriel. Take me to Loretto."

It was Gabriel's own wish. The same thought was in both their hearts. Loretto was farther off than Mount Gabriel, but they drove there slowly and in silence, and met the Colonel at the door. He had just returned from trout-fishing with Charlie. The Colonel frowned when he first caught sight of the pair, and muttered something unpleasantly between his teeth. But, on nearer view, the deadly pallor of the boy startled him.

"Great heaven! what has happened?" he exclaimed.

"The beginning of the end," said Gabriel.

And Clarence looked up at him with dark shadows under his eyes and a fresh blood-stain on his lips that had not yet been quite removed.

"A hemorrhage," ejaculated the Colonel.

"Yes."

"Why did you bring him here? Why not take him home at once, where he would have Doctor Melville's constant attendance?"

"His home is here, for awhile at least," replied Gabriel. "He will not trouble you long, Colonel Cleverton."

The Colonel winced at this rebuke. He felt that he had been cruel. He was glad when his sister Mary appeared on the scene to relieve him. Mrs. Cleveland comprehended the situation at a glance. She still shrank from the boy, but her duty was clear. She conversed a moment apart with her brother.

"Of course," said the Colonel, "we are Christians, and can't do otherwise. But don't put him in *her* room, Mary, — not in *her* room."

"It is the only one ready."

"Give him my room, your room; but not *her* room."

The pale woman thought a moment, and then answered : —

"If God will let him into His rooms forever, brother, don't you think we might admit him awhile into ours, — even into that of Sister Agnes?"

The Colonel shrugged his shoulders, and Clarence soon found himself in the quiet chamber which had been preserved as Agnes left it. He divined at once whose room it was, and whispered to Gabriel : —

"I know where I am. I shall die here."

"So, my little man," said Dr. Melville that evening, "you have been over-exerting yourself with that restless Gabriel, and must be punished accordingly. I forbid any more walks and any more talks. You are to lie abed for a week and not speak above your breath. Then we'll take you home, if you are well enough, as I hope you will bè."

"I *am* home," said Clarence. "This is Sister Agnes' chamber. Doctor, will I live till she gets back?"

"I hope so."

"Will she bring my father with her?"

"I think so."

"Keep me alive till then, Doctor, if — if it is in your power."

"I will try, Clarence. We doctors can't do as much as they think we can, but we can still do something, with God's help. I shall be almost constantly with you until you are better"——

Or worse," added Clarence, smiling, for there was a cadence in the doctor's voice which implied a reservation.

Clarence grew worse. It was a rapid decline, a vanishing away. He was dying of sheer loss of blood. Nothing could stop it. The Colonel grew fond of the uncomplaining boy, and sometimes wept a little to see how fast the handkerchief changed from white to crimson. Mrs. Cleveland was always at the bedside unless relieved by Lel or Gabriel. But Clarence missed a something in her look he longed for, and fancied she still shrank from him. Once when they were alone, and she had propped him on the pillows so that he could see the convent spires, he said to her : —

"I want to ask you something, but I'm afraid to."

"Afraid of what?"

"Of offending you."

"I shall not be offended, Clarence. Ask me."

"Will you kiss me when I'm dead ?"

She started and trembled.

"Why do you ask?"

"Because the stain will be off me then."

He thought she was offended, for she rose and turned hastily away. But the next instant she had fallen on her knees at the window, with her face buried in her hands. And this guarded, undemonstrative lady sobbed as though her heart would break as the one temptation which threatened her gentle heart disappeared forever. And in her deep contrition, she kissed the feet of the crucifix and prayed aloud that she might be forgiven her coldness to the motherless boy. The door opened and Gabriel stood over her with the triumphant smile of a seraph. But she saw him not, or heeded him not. She went straight to Clarence, bent over him, kissed him, and laid his head on her shoulder. There was no shrinking after that. She was all tenderness and love. Her very touch was different, and Clarence would fall asleep with his hand in hers, as happy as though the grave were not so near him. It was so to the end.

But the end was near; nearer than they thought. After being anointed by the confessor of the convent, he rallied so that it was hard to realize that he was dying.

"I should like to live," he said to Gabriel, "to see Sister Agnes and my father."

"They will be here to-morrow."

"I shall see them, then," exclaimed the boy, half rising in his bed.

"As God wills," answered Gabriel.

CHAPTER XXXIII.

CARRIAGE stood before the white palings of Loretto. The house was closed, the windows barred. It was all so still that you could only hear the humming of the bees. Charley came running to meet them, his eyes full of tears, his hands full of white roses, which he had just been gathering.

"Too late," murmured Agnes to herself, as she caught a glimpse of Lel's sad face in the doorway, and as Gabriel and Melville advanced to receive the Wanderer.

"Shall we assist you, sir," said Melville.

"You are very kind. I think I can walk with a little support. Let me try."

After a few steps toward the house he stopped as if to compose himself, and raising his eyes looked steadily around him. Twenty years since he saw that scene! He smiled to think how little it had changed. The sharp roof, the double portico, the red honeysuckles, were still the same. The double curve of the mountains was still there, like a Greek bow bent by a giant. It was a scene that had haunted him in all his wanderings — the home which his heart had never utterly forsaken — the solitude in which he had prayed to God to accord him a grave.

Yet how should he face the inmates of that silent house? He was nerved for trial, schooled by adversity, absorbed in the opening afterward, but he shuddered at the ordeal before him. It was not till Agnes whispered, "Courage, father," that he could ascend the steps.

"Is Clarence here?" he said to Melville.

"Yes."

The tone in which this was uttered revealed all.

"Let me see him," said the Wanderer, with a firmer voice, and walking without their aid.

It was but a step or two. The hall opened into the front parlor, and there lay Clarence between the lighted tapers of the dead, watched by Mrs. Cleveland and the Colonel. Long and tender was the gaze of the father at his son, and then raising both hands to heaven, he said, with an energy that thrilled them all: —

"I thank thee, O my Saviour, for this crowning mercy! It is thus I wished to meet him. Will you leave me here a moment with him — and his watchers," he added, glancing at the Colonel and Mrs Cleveland.

The three were hardly alone with the dead, before a deep voice, in its last wail, was heard even in the hall: "My wife — my friend — forgive me, in the name of God!" And with the kind answer came a falling sound that brought them all back into the room. The Wanderer was lying at Mrs. Cleveland's feet, the Colonel vainly trying to revive him. Nor did he answer when Agnes called him "Father."

"It is all over," whispered Melville to Lel.

And Gabriel, stooping over Clarence, as though the boy could hear him, whispered: —

"You will see your father now."

CHAPTER XXXIV.

THERE were two more graves on the hillside. Clarence and the Wanderer were sleeping side by side. Nor was their last resting-place forgotten or unadorned;

and when All Souls' Day came no other spot was richer in wreaths and flowers.

"It makes no difference even here," mused Gabriel, as he laid an ivy cross over the remains of his young friend. And looking up he saw Mr. Almy beside him.

"I was expecting you," continued Gabriel. "When did you arrive?"

"Last evening."

"Do you remain?"

"Awhile."

"Why not always?"

"I cannot be in two places at once.

"*Clarence is*"——

Mr. Almy started. The attack was so sharp and sudden.

"But I—I must be in town, or let my business go to the—dogs."

"So you prefer letting your soul go there?"

"Not quite that, I hope," said Almy, smiling.

"Quite that, *I know*," answered Gabriel. "Are you not rich enough yet?"

"Who is?"

"*They!*"—he pointed to the graves at their feet.

The leaves were falling around them, and light gusts of snow drifting over the mountain.

"And so the Wanderer died a happy death," resumed Mr. Almy, after a long pause.

"Let us hope so," said Gabriel.   "He will not be asked to pass through the eye of a needle, Mr. Almy.   His temptation was love, not money."

"Do you mean that money's mine?" asked Almy.

"One of yours."

"The other?"

"Wine."

"Is there any other?"

"*Not* whist," said Gabriel, remembering Lel. And then as Almy laughed, he added: "You are too old for such follies as these.   You will soon cease to be respectable if you pursue them, and I, for one, am already ashamed of you. Don't shrivel up into a wretched old worldling; I'd almost as soon see you an exemplary hypocrite.   Give up the world and stick to your daughter."

"That's easier said than done."

"Don't you love your daughter better than the world?"

"Possibly.   But I want a *new* affection.   I can't have it, I know; but the world affords variety at least.   A daughter married is a daughter lost."

"And yet parents are always glad to lose them until they *are* lost.   I thought you were above such common canting, but you turn out no better than the rest of them.   And Providence is going to humor you like a spoiled child, and give you your *new affection.* Let us see what it will do for you." And frowning half playfully, half scornfully, over his shoulder as he went, Gabriel passed through the gate and swept down the hillside.

"Such a famous rating I never yet received," said Almy to himself, "and the worst of it is that the fellow's right. Hang him, he's always right. I was half inclined to choke him, though, when he had the impudence to talk of Providence humoring me like a child; I wonder what he means? I think I can guess. Ah! these dead! I don't like our last home, or the way we get there. If it were only all safe beyond it! But it's not all safe by a good deal, and there's the everlasting rub."

And Mr. Almy mused among the decorated tombs until the quiet graveyard was white with snow, and the late dinner-call of the horn at Mount Gabriel summoned him back to his place among the living.

That very night a new soul was added to the number of the living whom he knew, and Mr. Almy found his new affection. To be a parent is the consummation of maturity; to be a grand-parent is the mysterious rejuvenescence of age. Just when the world is well found out, and the

heart has run the round of most human emotions;
when friends have passed or dropped away;
when children are absorbed in other loves and
other cares, and we find ourselves journeying
alone into the decline of life, comes this voice
from the cradle, sounding the resurrection of
our youth and assuring us of a new partnership
with the future.

Mr. Almy was not a sentimental man, not
addicted to idols of any sort. He had been
devoted to Lel, but it was in a rational, deliberate way. He had never been the passive slave
of any affection. He had laughed his full share
at the grand-parental mania. He remembered
how he had himself been adored in his day, to
his own serious detriment. He was amazed at
finding himself so deeply and incomprehensibly
interested in this second advent. She was a
beautiful child, to be sure, this girl of Lel's, but
not entirely without some resemblances to other
children. Very much like her mother at her
age, but then there was a halo round *her* head
which Lel had never worn. The mist of age,
like the morn of youth, makes its own aureole —
but he never thought of this. He considered
himself as young as ever, and so he was for all
practical purposes; but the heart is generally in
its dotage long before the head. His mind was

unimpaired, but his soul was already in its second childhood. It was wandering back in spirit from the confines of the coffin to the regions of the cradle.

The worst feature in his case was a growing jealousy of the parents. The girl properly belonged more to him than to them; *he* had the first right to her. They didn't, they couldn't love her as he did; they did'nt see the halo round her head as he did; they couldn't bring her up as he could; they certainly hadn't as much money to give her as he had. Why on earth wouldn't they make him her guardian on the spot, and renounce all interference henceforth and forever? Why wouldn't they both go away and leave her to him,—it was the least they could do. One thing he was bent on, however. They might be as selfish and despotic as they liked, and as parents are apt to be with another man's grandchild, but he *would* have the naming of her.

Melville had already fixed upon the name. She was to be called after her mother, of course; anything else would be monstrous. It was a name that nobody could or should object to. As for opposition from Mr. Almy, it never once occurred to him.

Mr. Almy knew this, and the evening before

the christening, when he and Melville were alone together, began his attack.

"What are you going to call her?"

"Lel, of course."

"Isn't one Lel enough? I don't like duplicates."

"It's a pity to let a family name die."

"You may have other opportunities of perpetuating it."

"What name would you like, sir?"

"Oh, it's not for me to decide. It's no affair of mine. I never meddle where I'm not wanted."

Melville smiled. Had the sharp merchant changed so? Was he such a baby already?

"Mrs. Melville wishes to see you, sir," called a servant. Lel had partly overheard the conversation and guessed the drift of it. She was laughing when her husband joined her.

"Let him have his own way, Melville."

"But really, Lel, I think that I might at least have the privilege of"——

"Being a sensible father instead of a goose of a grandfather. Grandfathers are always geese, Melville."

"But who knows what he may call her. Sophonista, may be."

"Oh no, not Sophonista"

"Cunegunda, then?"

"Nor Cunegunda, either."

"What then?"

"Just what I would call her if I had my way."

"Don't you want her called Lel?"

"No."

"The — deuce you don't. Well, madam, if not too inquisitive, may I venture to ask what you and your father *would* like to call her?"

"By a name that you have often admired."

"I admire none as much as yours."

"But I do; one name at least."

"What?"

"Don't you know the softest spot in my father's heart?"

"There it lies," pointing to the sleeping child.

"One softer than that?"

"No, I don't."

"Sister Agnes. Mind you, Melville, he's never said a word to me, but I'll bet you a hundred dollars he wants her called Agnes."

"And you want her called Agnes, too?"

"Yes."

"Agreed, though I don't."

Mr. Almy took no notice of Melville's return. He spoke of the graveyard, of the wheat-fields, of the Colonel, of Gabriel, of everything else than the baby.

"Well, sir," said Melville, "I surrender. My wife wishes you to have your own way."

"She is very kind, very," was the dry answer. "It is always charming in a daughter to let a father have his own way."

Melville laughed again. He was a father, too, and yet the pair of them wouldn't let him even name his own child.

"I wish to do nothing contrary to your wishes," continued Mr. Almy, with increasing dignity.

"I dare say you will name your granddaughter quite as prettily as you named your daughter. Lel is not the only pretty name in the world. Who will stand for her?"

"Why not Mrs. Cleveland and the Colonel?"

"An excellent idea."

"And why not, in compliment to them, — the Colonel would enjoy it so, — why not call her Agnes? I'm sure we all loved her."

"You have chosen the very name, sir."

"Shall it be Agnes, then?"

"With all our hearts, sir."

"Thank you, Melville." Mr. Almy wrung his hand and turned away to mount the stairs and have a look at his idol. He was satisfied. He had paid tribute to a holy thought that had crossed his heart like a bird of passage, crossed it without resting there. It had passed like a dream, but the idol of his later days should perpetuate a memory that stood starlike in the past, faint, pure, and sacred.

And so they called her Agnes, although her eyes and hair were like her mother's, and she promised to be Lel all over again. Mr. Almy could not persuade himself to leave her. His new affection enslaved him. Every post brought letters urging his return, which he would throw in the fire, always without answering, often without reading.

"I must go, Lel," he said at length, "and shan't be back till Christmas."

"We shall miss you dreadfully. What will Aggie do without you?" said this artful woman.

"What shall I do without her, you mean? The little humbug doesn't even know who I am. Lel, I am making a great ass of myself over this blooming little brat, but I'll be hanged if I can help it."

"And so you'll not be back till Christmas?"

"Not till Christmas."

But Mr. Almy was back in a fortnight, saying, by way of excuse, —

"Those old fellows bore me so with their bluff that I've had to run from them. Can't we have a whist party here? I'm sure the Colonel will

join. They are lonely enough at Loretto, and
we're not so very far apart."

The Colonel was only too glad of the chance,
and so even was Mrs. Cleveland, for the shadow
had been swept from her life, and with its
departure the capacity for joy revived. Mr.,
Almy began to find himself contented in the
country, and considerably weaned from town.
He even hinted at retiring from business. But
he was determined not to be precipitate. He
tested himself first with the Colonel. They were
both good shots, and there was no end of partridge and pheasant, or quail and partridge. He
had been fond of shooting once, and soon found
out that he was fond of it again. They were
both wretched anglers, and that was another
bond between them, as they both fancied themselves proficients. Charley often had a sly laugh
at the pair as they sat beneath the hemlocks.

By the time Christmas came the Colonel and
Mrs. Cleveland were so thoroughly domesticated
at Mount Gabriel that they determined to have
their Christmas celebration there instead of at
home. The presents were arranged for distribution to all comers, and the porches festooned
with spruce and pine and cedar in the most
artistic way. Almy was expected the day before, and kept his word, bringing with him two

trunks full of toys for the unsuspecting and unthankful young Agnes. The snow was a foot deep, and there was but an hour of daylight when he arrived, yet he and the Colonel sallied out together, afoot, on what was evidently a mysterious and important errand. In one of their recent hunts they had noticed a superb young hemlock spruce, and devoted it in their heart of hearts to a Christmas Bush. They felled the beautiful creature between them, and away they went, staggering through the snow and the bitter wind, dragging their prize after them, as happy as two boys. Such a Christmas bush was never seen in all that country. And when it was all decked and lighted, and the room was thronged with girls and boys from leagues around, on Christmas night, and the cake and egg-nog were passed around, little Agnes crowed and laughed as if she really enjoyed the festival.

When another Christmas came, and Mr. Almy arrived, with *three* trunks this time, Miss Aggie had been trained to walk to meet him, and say, "*Gan'pa.*"

"Confound it," said Almy, "can such nonsense make a man cry? Did you *teach* her to say 'Gan'pa,' Lel, or did she take to it naturally?"

"Oh, naturally, of course," said Lel, dropping her eyes.

"Don't laugh at me, Lel. I know I'm ridic-ulous, but with all that it's a splendid sensation. May you live to enjoy it."

And that evening he said to her, "You gave me a surprise to-day, so I shall give you one. to-night. I have turned over my house to my partners, and withdrawn absolutely. It is what I have been aiming at for two years, and is now accomplished. I'll live with you, if you'll let me, and if we get tired of each other we'll go abroad once in a while."

Lel delayed her answer, the tears were running down her cheeks so fast.

"This *is* a Christmas gift," she said, at length. "You have given me yourself, you grand old silly, splendid father, and if I ever let you take back the gift"——

"May he never have another new affection," chimed in Gabriel. "Ah, Almy, if I could only manage the Colonel as easily as your grandchild manages you!"

CHAPTER XXXV.

HE death of the Wanderer had made a deep but not a lasting impression on the Colonel. He was hale and hearty; there was many a good, quiet year before him;

he had time enough to make his peace with God, and die as good a Catholic as any of them. The Wanderer had profited by the last moment; why need *he* be in a hurry? He had no crimes on his conscience. He had never been a scandal like Cleveland, or a worldling like Almy.

But that very winter the admonition came. A sudden shock passed over him at night, and he rose a changed man in the morning. He tried to conceal it, but the ruin would not be hidden. One afternoon, as he lay dozing before the fire, Charley came rushing in with glistening eyes.

"Oh, sir, what a flock of partridges I saw! If I'd only had the gun I could have killed twenty at a shot. They were all huddled up in a bunch in the fence corner by the quarry. And——" Charley stopped short, for a tear was rolling down the old man's cheek.

"Come, Charley, we'll have a look at them, anyhow. I think a walk will do me good. We'll give them a round to-morrow."

And so they sallied forth together, without the gun, however; it would have puzzled the Colonel to carry it, although his pace was so rapid that the boy stared in amazement. The Colonel was not thinking of the birds. His eyes were bent on the ground; but occasionally he raised them, and they rested awhile on the slender spire of tho convent, towards which he was hastening.

"Now, sir," cried Charley, as they drew near the quarry, "I'll show you where they are."

"To-morrow," said the old man, raising his stick, and pointing to the spire. "This way, now."

They kept on their way in silence. In vain the ploughman bowed and the red-cheeked dairy-maid curtsied to the Colonel as they passed; he heeded them not, he saw them not, he knew them not. They were puppets, nothing more; things apparently near, but really at an infinite distance. Charley, amazed at such unusual abstraction and discourtesy, began to suspect him of sudden insanity, and trembled. They reached the gate; they stood by the church. It was Saturday afternoon, and sweet voices were singing the Litany of Loretto. The Colonel paused awhile, as if to inhale the melody and the keen, fresh air. The sun was just behind the mountain, and all along the west the graceful outlines of those blue ridges were marked in crimson and gold.

"The service is over," muttered the Colonel, as the organ ceased. "I must lose no time." He crossed the sloping terrace and rang the bell. "Wait for me, Charley."

"My niece," said the Colonel to the portress. "I wish to see her for a few minutes." Sister Agnes soon appeared, smiling. A year had changed her much; she was thinner and paler than before, but every feature and every action expressed perfect peace. Whatever had been the struggle, it was over; there was nothing left but the Sister of Charity, the meek servant of God. From the moment she entered the room, the Colonel's eye never left her; and though she had not at first remarked his agitation she soon saw that he was almost supernaturally excited.

"Agnes," said the Colonel, "I am breaking to pieces, crumbling away, I cannot last much longer. I am going to leave you, Agnes, going to leave you forever. I am near the end of a long, unworthy life; and while I can yet speak, I have a duty to perform which I must now discharge. I cannot rest until I have said that my opposition to your choice was the miserable result of selfishness and folly; and that I now thank God, and bless you, for the defeat of my most unmanly schemes!"

The old man rose from the chair, as if lightened of some crushing weight.

"But to leave you, Agnes — you whom I have loved so blindly that I was envious even of Him to whom your soul belonged, — to part for all eternity from — No! no! — Agnes, Agnes! tell me, have I yet time to meet you in Heaven?"

She said not a word, but grasped his hand and led him into the church. There on the cold marble aisle knelt the old man, trembling and sobbing, his head bowed to the step of the sanctuary, whilst kneeling like an angel beside him, his Agnes whispered, —

"Think not of me, but of God!"

She left him an instant, and passed into the sacristy. A moment and she reappeared, followed by a figure in black — and the priest waited in the confessional. Three paces off stood the tribunal of remission and the minister of absolution!

"Not now!" said the Colonel, shuddering, and refusing her mute petition. "Not now — *to-morrow!*"

"To-morrow may never come!" replied Agnes; "falter not at the foot of the altar!"

He rose and wavered — the sisters were coming — "To-morrow, to-morrow, I am unworthy now!" — and as the confessor advanced towards him he shook off Agnes, who still clung to him, and left the church.

The Colonel walked more rapidly than before, and as he passed the quiet graveyard the leafless branches seemed to creak, "*Like a thief in the night! Like a thief in the night!*" Once more he turned towards the convent, and a figure like Gabriel's stood an instant in the road, beckoning him back. But he sighed to himself

"to-morrow, to-morrow," and· at last the spire of
the convent sank behind the trees. Then the
road grew dark at his feet; but when he looked
up the moon was shining, unprofaned by a single
cloud, and all the stars were joyfully twinkling.

"Are you tired, sir?" asked Charley, as they
opened the white gate of Loretto. But before
there·was time for a reply Gabriel overtook
them.

"So you have really been following me," said
the Colonel. "I thought I caught a glimpse of
you."

Mrs. Cleveland, who had been anxiously watching in the porch, came to meet them.

"Sister," said the Colonel, "I thought myself
a good, blameless man, but on reviewing my life
I find myself a traitor to my faith and a slave
to sin. To-morrow shall find me once more in
the bosom of the Catholic Church. One night of
preparation is all I ask. I have been with
Agnes!"

The delirious strength that had hitherto sustained him began to give way, and he leaned
heavily on his sister's arm. The secret was
soon unfolded to Lel, Melville, and Mr. Almy;
and, revived by the happy group around him,
the Colonel looked and felt better than he had
done for many a day. Mrs. Cleveland was over-

whelmed with joy at this sudden and unexpected change, and the last open wound of her heart was healing. Gabriel alone was sad and restless. He sat in a corner playing strange airs upon a guitar, with which he loved to give music lessons to the boy. They could distinguish at times, words like these, —

> A woodman said to a snow-white flower,
> "Lily, I'll pluck thee in an hour!"
> So merrily, merrily hied he on,
> And came in an hour — the lily was gone!

And Gabriel sang other songs, mournful and slow; but the words were of some strange language, which none of them understood.

After an hour, which passed in congratulation and prayer, the Colonel excused himself and retired to his room. Gabriel, unseen, glided in after him. Through the open window he could see the cross on the convent spire gleaming in the moonlight; he remembered the morning that Lel stood at that same window, when he tempted her to win Agnes to the world, to the world which he had exhausted, which left him nothing but tears and shame, which might separate him from Agnes eternally? Separation from Agnes was the point of his contrition. He was tempted to return and complete at once the work he had begun; but it seemed so childlike and cowardly to be hurrying after a confessor, as if afraid of darkness. So, with a resolute effort he closed the shutters, saying, "*To-morrow!*"

The next morning he came not down to breakfast. They heard a shriek from Gabriel, and rushed up-stairs. The Colonel was lying dead on the floor.

Oh, what a change had come over Gabriel! His smile was gone — a sad, unearthly light shone in his blue eye — he was worn away to a skeleton. He rarely spoke, but, when they questioned him, mournfully pointed to his heart — and they knew that the disease of which he had often complained, if one so gentle could be said to complain, was carrying him off. Once they heard him singing a strange song, which Lel remembered : —

I hear a sweet voice, like the voice of a bird,
The softest and sweetest that ever was heard,
And it comes from the sky, from the blue, blessed sky,
And it warbles — " Prepare, for the hour is nigh!"
  And that voice is meant for me —
    Far away, far away,
    Ere another day,
      Shall I be!

I see two sweet wings that are not of the earth,
That shall bear me aloft to the land of my birth,
Yes, two glittering wings of the purest white,
With each feather enshrined in a circle of light!
       And those wings are meant for me —
          Far away, far away,
          Ere another day,
             Shall I be!

The blossoming stars were my playmates of yore,
I shall walk the bright fields where I've sported before;
And I know a sweet spot where the angels are,
That is high above the highest star!
       And that spot is meant for me —
          Far away, far away,
          Ere another day,
             Shall I be!

And, after singing this, he seemed stronger, and more cheerful; his old smile returned, and he went forth alone.

The sun was down behind the gap in the mountain, the moon was shining on the porches of Loretto and Mount Gabriel, yet the pale youth returned not.

In the morning they searched the fields and hills for him in vain; until, at last, guided by little Charley, they found him *dead on the Colonel's grave!*